**"Cut the hau**

Infuriatingly, Lu
closer, crowdin
woman, but yo
glow of a woman in love."

Annie closed her eyes, fighting to control the feelings he was so heedlessly creating within her.

His next words, softly spoken but impregnated with deadly meaning, shocked her into total immobility. "You're far more sexually aware of me than you are of Norman. And don't deny it," he warned silkily, "or I might be tempted to prove it."

Then he smiled, very slowly, very sure of himself. "There's a pretty potent brand of chemistry between us—immediate and undeniable. And you know it. I saw the recognition in your eyes the first time we met. You panicked then and you're panicking now."

**DIANA HAMILTON** creates high-tension conflict that brings new life to traditional romance. Readers find her a welcome addition to Harlequin and look forward to new novels by this talented author.

## Books by Diana Hamilton

Don't miss any of our special offers. Write to us at the following address for information on our newest releases.

Harlequin Reader Service
P.O. Box 1397, Buffalo, NY 14240
Canadian address: P.O. Box 603,
Fort Erie, Ont. L2A 5X3

# DIANA HAMILTON

## passionate awakening

**Harlequin Books**

TORONTO • NEW YORK • LONDON
AMSTERDAM • PARIS • SYDNEY • HAMBURG
STOCKHOLM • ATHENS • TOKYO • MILAN

Harlequin Presents first edition July 1991
ISBN 0-373-11377-3

Original hardcover edition published in 1990
by Mills & Boon Limited

PASSIONATE AWAKENING

# CHAPTER ONE

SHE had never seen him before in her life and she didn't think she wanted to see him again.

He looked dangerous, Annie Ross thought sharply, instinctively stepping aside to avoid a collision as the dark-haired stranger closed the ancient, silvery oak door in the garden wall.

As she stood there, her feet planted wide on the broad pavement, staring at him with an unwilling gaze, she decided hazily that her velvety brown eyes must have registered something of her wild inner apprehension, because the slow, sexually assessing smile that had warmed the stranger's startling blue eyes and quirked the austere lines of his mouth gave way to a kind of laid-back query. And then he turned with a slight inclination of his head, his long, easy stride taking him to the gun-metal Ferrari parked in the quiet, tree-lined street.

Only when the roar of the exhaust shattered the warm afternoon silence did Annie release her pent-up breath. For some reason she was shaking.

But, stiffening her spine, she mentally dismissed the man she had almost collided with, dismissed his immediate and uncomfortable effect on her. Dangerous, indeed! she nagged at herself. She was being fanciful, and that wasn't like her. She pushed the door open, the sun-bleached wood warm and grainy beneath her fingers, and then rooted briskly in her soft leather shoulder-bag for the house key, her generous mouth twisting wryly. The key was on permanent loan from Chris Howard, Seabourne's only estate agent, and he had told Norman, 'You might as well give in gracefully, old chap. Annie's obviously set her heart on Monk's Hall, so you might as well start packing now.' And the three of them had laughed, knowing Chris was joking because Norman was set in his ways; he didn't like change.

But Annie hoped to alter all that. Surely she could be allowed some say in the matter of where she and Norman lived after their marriage? Her mouth, above a small rounded chin, took on the determined line that reflected her character, her eyes lifting to sweep over the elegantly proportioned Queen Anne house.

As always, when she closed the garden door behind her, there came the familiar feeling that she was coming home, entering a world within a world, an enclosed and secret place found only when one passed through the silvery oak door in the high garden wall. All around her the garden was wild and lush, hints of early autumn colour showing in leaves just turning gold and bronze.

'That you, Annie?' The male voice startled her, intruding as it did in this enchanted place, and she paused on the mossy path, pushing her tanned fingers through her stylishly layered, rich, Titian hair, a half-smile beginning to soften her coral-tinted mouth as she saw Chris Howard pocket his keys and advance slowly down the path towards her.

Chris was one of Norman's closest friends and had been the first to know of their engagement two months ago, and now he grinned. 'I might have known you couldn't keep away from the place!'

Annie thought that his grin looked strained today and she said, almost accusingly, 'You've been showing someone around,' which was childish of her because, after all, it was part of his job.

'That's right.' His light blue eyes avoided hers. 'The auction's only a week away—interest is bound to escalate sharply.'

From time to time she had encountered others who had been viewing the property. Some had been merely curious, others interested but apprehensive about the price the house could command at auction. The stranger she had seen coming through the garden gate would not be a time-waster, nor would a little thing like the possibly high price of a desirable property worry him. If she hadn't known that instinctively, then the car he drove, the clothes he wore, the easy aura of supreme self-confidence that clung to him like a second skin would have told her that much. He would be a man who knew exactly what he wanted and how to get it. And the wretch had taken up residence inside her head, spoiling her day.

She was about to ask 'Who is he?' then decided she didn't want to know and remarked instead, 'I'm going to have to twist Norman's arm over this.'

She was only half joking because, when they'd decided to marry, Norman had said, 'We'll live here. There's no point in moving when we have a ready-made home.' He and his first wife had moved into The Laurels on their marriage, and after her untimely death Norman had stayed on, employing a housekeeper, Joan, who was with him still.

'What is it about this place, for you?' Chris asked earnestly, sitting down on one of the stone benches that flanked the main door. 'You've been haunting the place ever since old Miss Jennings moved out and put it in my hands.'

'I know,' Annie agreed, a reluctant smile pulling at her mouth as she sank resignedly on to the sun-warmed stone beside him. She didn't like people digging into her motives—not even those as well known and well liked as Chris. But putting her feelings for Monk's Hall into words might make it easier for her to understand them herself.

'Just instinct, I suppose,' she began with a wry shrug of slender shoulders. She elaborated slowly, 'In the whole of my life I've never had a proper, settled home. Mother and I were always moving around.' Idly, she traced a pattern on the mossy path with the toe of one leather walking shoe, her deep brown eyes reflective. 'When I was a little girl I used to dream about having a real home, a beautiful house with my own room, a place where I could keep all my treasured possessions—the sort of things that give a child security and identity, the sort of things I was never allowed to keep for long because we were always moving on.'

'Were you an insecure, lonely child?' Chris questioned softly, and Annie gave a quick bright smile.

'Not at all. I was using general terms.' She had never lacked for material things. Her childhood had been one many an outsider would have envied. And there had always been plenty of people around.

'And Monk's Hall became an embodiment of those childhood dreams?'

'I suppose it must have done.' Annie's eyes were sparkling now. 'Three years ago, when I first set eyes on the house, I fell in love with it. It was shortly after I'd come here to work for Norman. I knew it was the type of house I'd always wanted. I knew I could live happily here for the rest of my life.'

'But not at The Laurels,' Chris stated, and Annie shrugged, not knowing, her eyes fixed on her hands as they lay curled together in her lap. The glint of the diamond Norman had given her made her feel like a traitor.

At thirty-nine Norman Welling was an historian of some repute, and when she had gone to work for him as his research assistant and secretary she had moved into The Laurels with him and his housekeeper. She had been invited to do so and it had seemed the sensible thing to do. And Annie was nothing if not sensible.

But she had disliked the unimaginative bungalow on sight, whereas the old Queen Anne house, overlooking the coast, had stolen her heart. And lately, each time she had come to wander through the achingly beautiful empty house, she had felt as if she were coming home.

But Chris said warningly, 'I wouldn't set my heart on it, if I were you. For one thing, it would take a bomb to get Norman to agree to move out of The Laurels, and for another——' he spread his hands '—there could be other bidders, just as keen as you.'

Meaning, Annie supposed acidly, the self-confident bastard she'd seen at the garden door.

'We'll see.' She gathered herself together, standing up in an unconsciously graceful, fluid movement. And, as Chris took his leave and she watched him walk away, she vowed to make one final, concerted effort to get Norman to agree to make the move.

With that unexpected legacy from a father she couldn't remember she could make an untoppable bid for Monk's Hall. She would willingly pay well over the odds. All Norman had to do was agree to leave The Laurels. It was as simple—and as difficult—as that.

Not that she would make a serious issue of it, though, she decided sensibly. Monk's Hall was the first thing they had ever even mildly disagreed about, and surely a house wasn't worth quarrelling over? On the other hand, she'd never made demands in all the time she'd known him, and Monk's Hall wasn't a shell of bricks and mortar. It could be the home she'd always longed for.

Quickly, she pushed aside that unbidden, half-angry thought and moved towards the main door. But the anticipation of again wandering through the house, planning how she would like to see it decorated, furnished, failed, for the first time ever, to give her the usual uplift of intense excitement.

The dark stranger and his unwanted interest in the house still occupied her mind, haunting it almost. The indefinable and quite probably fanciful aura of danger she had detected around him had imprinted itself on her mind. Just thinking of him made her skin sprout goosebumps! It was a stupid reaction, she told herself. But very real...

She was hot and out of sorts by the time she'd walked the two miles to the opposite side of town, to the quiet, modern suburb where she lived and worked with Norman. Her beige designer jeans and oyster cotton shirt were sticking to her and that made her feel uncomfortable.

Seabourne was an old fishing town, the small stone houses clinging like limpets to the sides of a shallow ravine, the narrow streets winding, steep in places.

The first time she'd seen Norman's home had been when she'd come for the job interview. She hadn't liked the large, functional bungalow then, and she didn't like it now. It was too neat, too lacking in character; it said nothing to her. And as far as Norman was concerned, he didn't seem to mind where he lived so long as he was comfortable, she thought, her straight, elegant nose wrinkling affectionately. Atmosphere didn't matter to him, but he disliked change. But if she could make him understand how she longed to own Monk's Hall, how easily she could make it a comfortable home, a home to be proud of, then surely he would agree to the move—for her sake?

Turning from the wide pavement to pass between The Laurels' gateposts, the hot autumn wind buffeting her, making her hair fly about her face, she stepped on to the short gravel drive and stopped dead in her tracks.

The gun-metal Ferrari parked directly in front of Norman's front door was unmistakable. Her stomach churned and, for a moment, she forgot to breathe. She couldn't imagine what that lean, dark stranger was doing here. The thought of him on her home territory made her hackles rise.

Hurrying now, which perhaps accounted for her breathlessness, she skirted the building and let herself in by the kitchen door. Joan was slicing bread, her smooth round face red and flustered, and the kettle was boiling its head off.

Annie unplugged it and tried to read Joan's mood. She had been Norman's housekeeper since his wife had died. In her late thirties, she could have been attractive if she had bothered about what she wore, how she did her hair. And until Norman had put the diamond ring on Annie's engagement finger she and Joan had rubbed along well. But recently Joan's moods had been unpredictable, to say the least, and Annie said lightly, 'There's a Ferrari parked outside. Visitors?' not voicing her real thoughts, which were, What the hell is that man doing here? Who is he? What's his game?

Joan would never have understood if she'd told her that something about the stranger's body chemistry had sparked off a bristling gut reaction deep inside her. No one would have understood it. She didn't even understand it herself.

'Some sort of distant cousin, I'm told.' Joan slapped butter on bread. 'Requiring tea and sandwiches.'

'Can I help?'

Annie didn't know if the extra chore was the cause of the housekeeper's ill humour or not. She was difficult to read these days, and Annie didn't know whether or not she was relieved when Joan said drily, 'No. Norman's been fussing because you're late. I suppose he wants to introduce you to this Luke Derringer. He'll be the first of the family to meet the prospective Mrs Welling.'

It was acidly said, but Annie had too much pride to let herself react. Her back straight, she walked out of the kitchen door and closed it gently behind her. Joan had been acting out of character ever since the engagement had been announced. Joan probably thought Annie wasn't good enough for their distinguished joint employer.

Mentally shelving the problem, Annie walked the length of the L-shaped corridor to the neat oblong bedroom that had been hers since she had come to work for Norman.

Reluctant to meet Luke Derringer face to face for the second time that day, she didn't hurry over making herself look more presentable. Norman hadn't many relatives, just a few distant cousins, and a spiteful fate had decreed that the Derringer man was one of them! She tucked a rust-coloured tailored silk shirt into the waistband of a classically styled, cream worsted skirt and wondered why the mere thought of him set her teeth on edge.

It could have nothing to do with the man personally, she informed herself with grim logic. It must be because she had instantly and instinctively recognised him as an achiever, a man who coolly and deliberately set out to get what he wanted. And if he wanted Monk's Hall he would do his damnedest to get it. Chris had as good as warned her of that, hadn't he? And that had to be the reason she had felt threatened when their eyes had met and held outside the garden door. Anything else was unthinkable.

Feeling unaccountably hot, Annie stared at herself in the mirror, wondering if the unusual inner turbulence showed through the cool outer veneer. She was tall and slim, self-possessed, her silky Titian hair skilfully layered around her oval, even-featured face. She had had years of practice in presenting the world with a face that kept its secrets, years of schooling her emotions. Ever since she could remember she had been trying to be as unlike her over-excitable mother as it was possible to be.

Satisfied that she presented her normal, poised image, she fished the car keys out of the pocket of her discarded jeans and went to find Norman.

'Sweetheart—you took your time!' There was reproof in Norman's voice, but only mild, and he was smiling as he got up from his chair behind the big leather-topped desk where he always worked.

A burly man, he would be forty next birthday, but his pale hair and stocky frame made him look older by much more than the six or seven years that must separate him from the tall, whippy stranger who was leaning against the broad windowsill, half sitting.

'I know.' Annie faced him, holding his eyes, her smile very cool, her voice light. Deliberately, she did not look Derringer's way. She was aware of him, though, terribly aware. And there was safety in the known; the respect and companionship she and Norman had built up over the years was comfortable, like an old, soft glove.

She put the keys she had been holding down on the desk.

'After I delivered the car for servicing I dropped by Monk's Hall,' she explained, cueing him into the conversation that would come later, when they were alone, and he grinned suddenly, his blunt, good-looking features looking almost boyish.

'That old place again!' His eyes twinkled, looking beyond Annie to the dark, silent man near the window. 'My fiancée's got a fixation lodged inside her pretty head—Annie, sweetheart, meet Luke Derringer—a kind of cousin, umpteen times removed.'

'We met earlier, outside Monk's Hall.' The deeply drawled statement set her teeth on edge, and Norman chuckled, his broad hands resting on Annie's slender shoulders, turning her round to face the stranger.

'That figures!' Norman's hands stayed on Annie's shoulders, holding her close, his fingers gently kneading the fine bones beneath the silk. Annie might have wondered at this unprecedented public display of affection had her mind not been on other things.

She was looking at Luke Derringer now, and he was looking at her, and the effect of those vivid blue eyes was catastrophic. He seemed to be asking silent questions—coming up with the answers, too—and when derision stared out at her from between thick black lashes she turned her head quickly, only just resisting the impulse to bury her face in Norman's comforting, sweater-clad chest.

Norman's arms tightened around her, almost as if he knew she needed protection, and as he questioned his cousin there was a strangely apologetic note in his voice which she sensed was for her benefit.

'Are you here for the auction, or just passing through?'

'For the auction.' Luke Derringer sounded very slightly amused as he pushed himself away from the windowsill. 'What else?'

What else indeed? Annie thought snidely, her huge brown eyes unwillingly drawn, watching Luke's easy, economical movements as he moved to where she and Norman stood. He wouldn't be here because of any family bond. One only had to look at that hard-boned face, those sardonic eyes, to know the man was a loner. Not for him the safety of the herd. He wouldn't have a sentimental bone in his lean, rangy body. No, he had somehow heard of Monk's Hall and he wouldn't have wasted his time coming down for the auction if he didn't intend walking away as the new owner.

'Unless it was to meet your future wife.' It was said with a cutting edge to the slightly husky voice, and Annie's eyes batted wide open as he bent his head, his intention clear, then her lashes fluttered closed at the shock of painful awareness as he touched his lips to hers.

That touch was light, the sensual movement of his teasing mouth sparking a chemistry that transformed her flesh to liquid fire, making her bones weak.

He hadn't said, 'Pleased to meet you at last,' or 'Welcome to the family,' or anything else that would have superficially excused that kiss. He'd just closed his mouth over hers, tasting her, his skin, his flesh, speaking to hers.

'You'll come to the wedding?' Norman asked tightly, as if the little scene hadn't amused him. And it hadn't amused Annie, either, not one bit. She felt shattered, almost besmirched, oddly out of control for the first time since she was seventeen years old. No way could she pass the incident off with her usual poise, say something like 'Happy to know you, cousin-to-be.'

She wanted to rub her hands over her mouth, to wipe away the memory of his vile touch, but she couldn't do that because it might hurt Norman and that was something she never wanted to do. He was kind and good and very dear to her.

'And when is the wedding?' Luke was asking her, his eyes hard and probing. Norman might not have existed.

She said thickly, 'We haven't decided yet, but soon,' and wondered why she'd made that qualification, because they'd tentatively set the date for next spring.

Turning quickly as the door opened, she hurried to help Joan with the laden tray, relieved by the distraction. But her hands shook as she poured tea while Joan passed sandwiches, and that was because Luke Derringer was there, disrupting the normal peace with vibrations that charged the air with ultra-potent electricity.

Distractedly, she glanced at Joan who had now taken her customary place behind the big silver teapot. She looked calm, as placid as ever, and Norman was now his usual affable self, talking to Luke, catching up on the news of their far-flung relatives.

So she was the only person to be affected by the highly charged atmosphere, the strangely electrifying presence of Luke Derringer. And when she heard Norman say, 'If you're staying around until the auction we can put you up here,' she could have screamed. She didn't know why she didn't want him near her, she only knew she didn't.

Helping Joan to make up the bed in the guest-room, Annie tried to pull herself together. She didn't understand what was happening to her. One look from

Luke Derringer's eyes was enough to take her breath away.

Joan, plumping pillows, said, 'What a dish that man is! He's the sort you don't expect to see this side of a film screen. I bet he's lost count of the broken hearts he's left in his wake.'

'If you say so,' Annie replied woodenly, her heart picking up speed. She had been trying to rationalise her reaction to Luke, to tell herself that it was solely due to his interest in Monk's Hall. But Joan's words had pointed her thoughts in another direction entirely, a direction that alarmed her.

Luke Derringer was a dangerously attractive man, and this was the first time in seven years that she had recognised the dangerous sexual attraction in a man.

For a moment she stood in shocked stillness, tall and slender, her radiant hair turned to a nimbus of gold in the rays of the late afternoon sun which slanted through the windows. The danger she had sensed in Luke was now explained, understood.

Unconsciously, she squared her shoulders. She could cope with that, couldn't she? She hadn't spent her formative years with a mother who went through husbands and lovers like a child goes through ice-creams on a hot day for nothing!

Her mother, a talented and beautiful actress, only came alive when a new man crossed her horizon. 'Falling in love,' she called it, but Annie had another, less romantic name for it and had learned to have a wary distrust for that particular kind of passion. It quickly burned itself out.

'Of course, you've got a husband lined up, so you could hardly admit to noticing that Luke has enough sex appeal to blow your socks off,' Joan commented tartly, and, watching the older woman sweep out of the room Annie wondered, not for the first time, if Joan's touchiness owed its existence to jealousy.

Joan had worked for Norman for longer than Annie had, and when she had been accepted for the research assistant-cum-secretary job Norman had said, 'We're a team here, Joan and I, and I know you're going to fit in with us. Welcome to the family!'

Sighing, Annie followed Joan out of the room. She was sorry if the other woman had been secretly in love with their boss for years, had harboured thoughts of becoming the second Mrs Welling. But there was nothing to be done about it, and she had more important things to think of right now. Now was as good a time as any to tackle Norman again about Monk's Hall.

At least Luke was out of the way. After he'd accepted the offer of a room—with indecent haste, Annie had thought—he had informed them easily, 'I have to go back to town—people to see. I shouldn't be late.'

And that, for Annie, had seemed to sum him up: laid-back and cool, doing his own thing—but charmingly. And no doubt the people he wanted to see were the agents handling the sale of Monk's Hall. For a moment she had been tempted to phone

Chris Howard, but common sense had prevailed. Monk's Hall would go to the highest bidder.

As was usual at this time of day Norman was relaxing with a pre-dinner sherry in the comfortable, traditionally furnished living-room, an erudite tome in his hands. She could pinpoint his exact activity at any given time of the day, she thought fondly. His predictability didn't bore her; it made her feel safe, and she was astute enough to recognise that this was a direct result of a childhood where she hadn't known from one week to another where she would be, or from one day to the next what her mother's mood would be—gay, tempestuous, or near suicidal—depending, as ever, on the state of her love life!

Norman lay aside his book, his pleasant features lighting up as she walked quickly over the rose-patterned carpet and perched on the arm of the chintz-covered chair he was using.

'Sherry, darling?' He made to rise, but she checked him with a slim, detaining hand on his arm.

'Later, perhaps. I'd like to talk.' And I'd like to creep on your lap and be cuddled, like a child. The thought came from nowhere, surprising her.

Their relationship wasn't physical, it was based on mutual respect and liking, on their logical desire for a secure and settled home life. Norman had a low sex drive, but that didn't really worry Annie. Surely the more stable feelings, such as respect and warm affection, were safer than the wild passion that produced the unthinking behaviour her mother had always indulged in?

'It's about Monk's Hall, isn't it?' He had finished his sherry, and he put his glass down on a
side-table as Annie smiled at him, her eyes wry.

'Am I so easy to read?'

'Not really.' He chuckled at her expression. 'But
you've had this bee in your bonnet ever since the
place came up for sale and your father, providen-
tially, left you a great deal of money. I was just
making an educated guess.'

'I fell for the place at first sight,' she admitted,
pulling a long face because he knew, and she knew,
that that kind of impulse was out of character for
her. 'What are your objections to the place?'

'To the house itself, none. But I'm lazy, I
suppose, I don't like change. Too set in my ways—
too old for you?' Sudden concern darkened his
eyes.

She said quickly. 'Rats! What's fifteen years?
Anyway, I prefer older men.' She must do, or she
would never have agreed to marry him. And if he
was set in his ways then that was OK by her because
she appreciated stability, order.

'Thank you.' The hand he placed over hers was
comforting. Getting to his feet, he squeezed her
fingers briefly. 'Put in your bid for Monk's Hall,
if it makes you happy. If you get it, I'll fork out
for any work that needs doing, out of whatever I
get for this place. Fair?'

She was so taken aback by this sudden, total ca-
pitulation that she couldn't find words to tell him
of her delight, her gratitude. She had expected an
outright refusal to budge on the issue, a reasoned

and logical argument explaining that selling up here and moving to Monk's Hall would be a retrograde step, a whole load of unnecessary hassle.

So she simply stared at him with glowing brown velvet eyes. She had misjudged him. She had steeled herself to hear him say that her passion for the old house on the coast was an aberration, a hiccup in the otherwise orderly workings of her mind. And she would reluctantly have had to agree with him.

'Would you like that drink now?' He was replenishing his own glass from the drinks tray and she shook her head, still speechless as she moved quickly across the room, her thick dark lashes spiked with tears of sheer happiness. He was an absolute poppet and she would make Monk's Hall a beautiful home for the two of them, a happy, secure place for their children to grow up in.

Emotionally, she flung her arms around him.

'Thank you, darling. The last thing I wanted to do was fight with you over where we should live. Thank you for understanding!'

'That's quite—quite all right,' he replied heavily, gently putting her aside. His bluntly good-looking features were red with embarrassment as he returned his attention to the sherry bottle. 'About that drink——'

'No, thanks,' Annie answered snippily. She felt hurt, like a dog who'd been kicked out into the cold. Norman hated emotional scenes, or anything remotely approaching them. Her calmness, the logical way she ordered her life, had been the first thing that had attracted him to her. He'd told her as much. But surely she could be allowed to express truly felt emotion once in a while?

'I'll go and see if I can help Joan with dinner,' she excused herself bleakly. For the first time ever a niggle of doubt about their relationship entered her mind.

But Joan, chopping mint for sauce, said, 'Everything's under control here, but if you'd fetch the washing in I'd be grateful,' and Annie escaped thankfully, glad to have a few moments on her own.

Unpegging bath towels, she decided wryly that Monk's Hall must have touched a vulnerable spot inside her, a spot so well hidden that she hadn't fully realised she had it. She had never felt passionately about anyone or anything until she'd set eyes on that house. She didn't count the painful episode with Hernando Carreras seven years ago. That was something she had learned from and put firmly to the back of her mind, yet never quite forgotten because the lesson she'd learned at seventeen had been salutary. But she wasn't ashamed of emotion and she didn't see why a natural display of affection should have embarrassed Norman. She didn't think it augured well for the future.

'You have a delectable nose, and I swear there's a blackbird about!'

She would have known that deep, husky voice anywhere and she went rigid, clutching the towels to her chest, not turning. She stood very still, but she was quivering inside. He had a terrible effect on her. But she did manage,

'I'm taking down the clothes, not hanging them out.' Her voice was creditably cool and steady. He had moved into her line of vision now, and the startlingly blue eyes seemed even more vivid out here, the thick hair darker, with a sheen like a raven's wing. And his mouth was teasing, softer than she remembered it, and she closed her eyes because looking at him completed a chemical reaction that sparked off an explosion deep inside her.

'And of course you won't be the maid much longer,' he remarked, his voice as dry as dust. 'You'll be queening it in the parlour. Do you like bread and honey—or do your tastes run more to caviar?'

'Are you trying to say something?' she rasped, gathering up the last of the towels. The allusion wasn't lost on her and she could cheerfully have hit him.

'Maybe.' A strongly defined dark eyebrow tilted upwards and the sensually wide mouth curled, revealing white, even teeth. 'Or maybe I'm wondering why a woman like you should be marrying a man like Cousin Norman. Security, is it?'

She dragged in a sharp shallow breath, her heart pattering wildly under her breastbone. He had moved in front of her, blocking the path, and to get past him she would have had to step on to Norman's neat rows of french beans. Her arms tightened around the bundle of towels. They smelt of fresh air and sunshine and, faintly, of fabric conditioner, and yet did nothing to mask the raw scent of masculine sexuality which this man seemed to exude from every pore.

'I find that remark thoroughly objectionable.' Her chin came up and her narrowed eyes glittered darkly, although she did manage to keep her voice coolly dismissive, masking her anger.

Infuriatingly, he chuckled. 'Cut the haughty act, Annie.' And he moved closer, crowding her, making her stomach churn, and a strong, tanned hand moved, lean fingers cupping her chin, setting her skin on fire, making her flesh pulse with unbearable sensation.

She jerked her head back savagely, sending silky Titian strands flying about her head, bright colour to balance the hectic scarlet that stained her cheekbones, darkening her eyes to jet. But, effortlessly, his fingers tightened, calmly stilling her frantic movements, holding her head rigid.

Stingingly, she was aware of the imprint of his fingers, of the slow, hypnotic movement of his thumb, moving with erotic lightness against her cheekbone, feathering her skin with searing sensation. Blindly, she closed her eyes, fighting to control the force of the feelings he was so heedlessly creating within her. She was shamingly aware of the way her lips were quivering, as if in invitation, and was unable to do anything about it.

'You are a beautiful woman,' he imparted, a wry note in his husky voice. 'But you lack that vibrancy, the glow that marks a woman in love.' His fingers tightened fractionally, making her eyes fly open, his own holding her unwilling gaze with aquamarine intensity. 'You're not in love with Norman and yet you've agreed to marry him. Don't blame me if I draw my own conclusions.'

She almost spat at him then, but his next words, softly spoken but impregnated with deadly meaning, shocked her into total immobility.

'You're far more sexually aware of me than you are of him. And don't deny it,' he warned silkily, 'or I might be tempted to prove it.'

Then he smiled, very slow, very sure of himself. 'There's a pretty potent brand of chemistry between us—immediate and undeniable. And you know it. I saw the recognition in your eyes the first time we met, outside Monk's Hall. You panicked then and you're panicking now.'

# CHAPTER TWO

ANNIE buckled the belt of her jeans and pulled on a lightweight wool sweater. She had never felt so tense. Although she had carefully avoided Luke for the past few days, he was still getting to her. The mere knowledge that he was under the same roof, breathing the same air, was enough to make her skin prickle, her stomach churn with awareness of him. Pushing her fingers through the silky fire of her hair she took several deep, relaxing breaths.

On the whole she was pleased with her performance. Never by word or look had she allowed her dislike and distrust of Luke to show through. During mealtimes, when she had had no option but to endure his hateful company, she had devoted her entire attention to Norman. Fortunately, Norman always worked in the mornings and she worked with him, and in the afternoons he liked to potter in the garden. He took quiet satisfaction from his neat lawns, his productive vegetable patch.

Normally Annie would spend her afternoons helping Joan around the house, shopping, catching up on her typing. But since Luke's arrival she had clung very close to Norman, feeling safe with him, although why she should feel under very real threat in Luke's company she didn't altogether know. She would be glad when he was gone.

The knowledge that he was a firm rival for the ownership of Monk's Hall was bad enough, but the way he had told her that in his warped opinion she was marrying Norman for financial security had been rudeness of the most objectionable kind.

She refused even to consider his effrontery in stating that they had some kind of sexual chemistry going for them. The wretched man didn't know what he was talking about! Instant sexual attraction didn't exist for her. Surely it didn't? It couldn't! She was far too level-headed.

Norman was waiting for her in the kitchen and his eyes lit up. 'Ready for work?' He pushed his stockinged feet into gardening boots and Annie's features softened in a fond smile. Dressed in heavy brown cords and a chunky zipped cardigan Joan had knitted for him years ago, he looked like a cuddly teddy-bear.

Joan, taking pots from the dishwasher, remarked tartly, 'If you're getting the beetroot up, bring a few roots to the kitchen. I'll make that pickle you're so fond of.'

'Will do!' Norman rubbed his hands together. He and Joan shared the same squirrel-like instinct, never happier than when they were storing or preserving the products of summer against the bleak, unproductive months ahead.

Outside, Norman took deep gulps of the sparklingly fresh autumn air. 'I'm glad you're taking an interest in the garden, Annie. It was the one thing I didn't think we had in common.' She smiled faintly, not liking to tell him that she would have clung on to his company, whatever he had been doing, because she needed him as a buffer against his cousin.

Instead she told him, 'I'm looking forward to next week.'

He answered slowly, 'So am I, in a way. It's a new departure, though.'

'I know.' She gave his arm a reassuring squeeze. Norman's books were heavily factual, every detail researched, checked and cross-checked. When she had half-jokingly suggested that he indulge in a little light relief—do a book based on historical legend as apart from historical fact—she hadn't really expected him to agree. But perhaps her enthusiasm had fired his. She sometimes felt, though, that she had pushed him into the project. Now she said, 'Two days in Wales with Professor Rhys should be stimulating.' But what she really meant was that by then the auction would be over and she would be able to relax, secure in the knowledge that she and Norman were the new owners of Monk's Hall and that Luke Derringer had left Seabourne, with luck never to return.

Norman nodded. 'Rhys is a reputable and highly respected source on the Merlin legends. Coupled with our own research into the Arthurian fantasy, his contribution will be invaluable.'

She took the tools he was handing her from the garden shed and was about to agree with his statement when she heard the unmistakable roar of the Ferrari's exhaust. Her head jerked up, her nostrils flaring as she breathed the crisp air, like an animal scenting danger, only relaxing when she realised that the powerful car, with its daunting driver, was leaving, not arriving.

'That cousin of mine never did learn how to relax,' Norman offered, watching the Ferrari exit between the gateposts. 'He's always going somewhere in a hurry—got to be head of the pack. Oh, and by the way' —his eyes had fallen on the heavy teak garden seat, set beneath the solitary tree— 'we'll move that seat on Saturday afternoon. Put it on the terrace; it will get more sun there.'

The auction was to be held on Saturday morning, so Annie didn't think the position of the seat relevant. After all, by next summer she and Norman would be beginning their married life together at Monk's Hall—of that she was very sure. So she said nothing, following as he trundled the wheelbarrow down the path, and when Norman said, 'What do you think of him?' she didn't know whom he was talking about. Her mind had been on that auction and the sense of glorious achievement that would be hers after she had made her successful bid.

'I haven't given him much thought,' she lied as soon as she'd decided Luke was the subject under discussion.

Norman said sourly, 'Then you must be a one-off. Women have been thinking of nothing but him ever since he reached eighteen!'

'He never married?' Annie queried, unwilling to be drawn into any conversation centred around Luke, yet perversely fuelling it.

Norman shrugged. 'Ten years ago he was too busy making his first million to have time for thinking of settling down. Too busy to want to make a serious commitment. And later, well...' his mouth drooped distastefully '...I suppose he realised he was on to a good thing. He'd been used to having affairs—a succession of sophisticated women moving through his life the way the seasons move through the year.' He tugged on his gardening gloves, his expression disgusted. 'I can't approve of that kind of shallow behaviour.'

'No,' Annie nodded, tight-lipped. That made two of them! 'So you don't think he'll ever settle down?'

'Pigs might fly!' Norman grunted. 'He long since discovered he could take his pleasures as and when it suited him, no regrets—no strings. Having to remain faithful to one woman for the rest of his life would bore him mindless.' He drove the fork into the ground, lifting a clump of prize-sized beets. 'His values are not ours, Annie, my dear. He's a bit of a cynic, too; he likes to travel light, far and fast, and, most of all, alone.'

'And his job?' Norman's information came as no surprise. She had already, intuitively, had him pegged as a loner, a hard man, sufficient unto himself. A shallow womaniser—hadn't his blatant sexual overture to her, his own cousin's fiancée, given her proof of that? She quite expected Norman to tell her, He's a wheeler-dealer. Something in the world of high finance, just this side of the law. But what he did say shook her, rooted her feet to the ground.

'He's in the hotel business in a big way. He's got strings of them—the sort that cost an arm and a leg just to walk through the foyer. Not my cup of tea.' He was dismissive. 'They're mostly situated abroad, where the very rich go to play, but lately— so he tells me—he's moving into the UK, buying up period property and——' He bit his words back, as if only just realising he'd said too much. Then he added, quickly and gruffly, 'Let's get a move on. It looks as if we'll have a good crop of beets this year, even better than last.'

Silently, she watched him work for a few moments. Her body was rigid, as still as if it were carved from stone. But her mind was racing.

So that was it. Luke Derringer wouldn't be wasting his time in a quiet backwater like Seabourne if cash registers weren't pinging in his ears! He liked to travel, fast and light. He wouldn't be interested in Monk's Hall as a home. Oh, no, it was to be one of his first UK projects! A gracious, select hotel for those who preferred a luxurious, peaceful holiday? A prestigious retreat for those of the very rich who had outgrown the glitz and glamour of jet-set playgrounds?

She raised her delicately curved chin, her nostrils dilating. Not if she could help it!

'I'll give you a lift.' It was a statement, not a suggestion, and as always that deep, slightly husky voice made Annie's spine tingle.

'No, thank you.' She had been adjusting the jade silk scarf she was wearing with a collarless, slim-fitting, dark grey suit, and she turned from the small hall mirror and looked straight through him.

She could be very good at looking through people if she really put her mind to it, but, to her intense annoyance, he merely laughed. It was a rich sound, deep in his throat.

Predictably, infuriatingly, her pulses began to race. He had a terrible effect on her senses, and the worst of it was, he knew it! No, she corrected herself—not the absolute worst. She simply didn't know what to do about it, and there could be nothing worse than that. Despite knowing exactly what a shallow heel he was—that knowledge springing from her own intuition and his cousin's lips—the philandering devil still had the power to make her quake inside. He still haunted her mind, waking or sleeping!

He considered her, his head slightly on one side, half smiling.

'Why not? We're both going to the auction. Pointless to take two cars.' The smile widened, touching his eyes, making them sparkle like precious gems. 'I'll give you lunch afterwards.'

The hell you will! she screamed at him in her mind. If small doses of him affected her so strangely she couldn't bear to contemplate what an intimate lunch for two would do! And it would be intimate, she knew he'd make sure of that. He'd been se-ducing her with his eyes ever since he'd arrived. And as he was Norman's guest—not to mention the fact that he was also Norman's cousin—it was particularly reprehensible.

'How kind!' she snapped sarcastically, reaching for her grey suede handbag, tucking it under her arm like a weapon. 'I have far too many things to do. In any case, I would prefer to have my lunch here, with my fiancé.'

'Why so antagonistic?' He calmly removed the handbag from her clutching fingers and replaced it on the telephone-table, asking huskily, 'Do you know? Or would you like me to tell you?'

He lifted a leisurely hand to her face, his fingers lightly touching her skin. Annie flinched, her eyes widening as they winged up to meet his. The blue was startling, vivid, deep, and she felt as if she were drowning, while that husky voice was having a shamefully disastrous effect on her, hypnotic almost.

'I wanted you from the first,' he told her silkily. 'And you know it. It was an instant reaction—a chemical response—call it what you will, but it was there. And you felt it, too. But you're denying it, fighting it. And so you translate all that emotion into antagonism.'

His words appalled the part of her mind that was still capable of logical thought. She tried to speak, to deny his every shaming word, but hot sensation flooded through her, drying her mouth, clogging her throat.

He was close and coming closer, and she managed to croak, 'Don't!' but didn't manage to move. She couldn't move, despite the thumping of adrenalin through her veins. She knew he was going to kiss her.

He had leaned forward, the intention clear in his eyes, in the sensual softening of the hard, incised mouth, and there was nothing, nothing at all she could do to prevent it. Something long buried, something primitive and undeniable, had surfaced, taking her over. Hazily, her eyes focused on his mouth.

As he kissed her, her eyes closed helplessly. She had no will-power left, none at all, as her lips parted willingly beneath the searching pressure of his. Desire came in a relentless flood, sweeping her away like a mindless weakling. Norman's occasional, undemanding kisses left her feeling warm inside, comforted. This was elemental, burning her up.

Physical need, too familiar to be disguised, propelled her hands to slide over the width of his shoulders, curving around his neck, twining through the crisp dark hairs at the nape of his neck, and, groaning softly, he deepened the kiss, fusing them together in this single, basic need.

Then, abruptly, he released her, drawing away, his eyes glittering with some nameless emotion as he said raggedly, 'Deny what there is between us, and you're a liar.' Then he walked away, leaving her shaken and stunned.

She didn't know how she drove to Monk's Hall without wrecking the runabout she and Joan shared. She felt mangled inside with sheer, blistering rage.

He would never have dared to kiss her like that, say the things he'd said, had anyone else been in the house. But Norman, unaccountably, had elected to go with Joan into town to pick up the weekend shopping—much to Joan's unconcealed delight and her own annoyance.

She had expected him to attend the auction with her—it was their future home that was going under the hammer, when all was said and done! And he might have known she would need his moral support because that louse Luke would be there, putting his bids in!

But no—oh, no! She crunched through gears and almost stalled the engine. He had decided to accompany Joan, as if she needed all the help she could get and hadn't been doing the weekend shopping for years!

So Norman had left her alone with Luke and Luke had kissed her. That made her very angry. That his kiss had filled her, body and soul, with burning sensation made her angrier still! She disgusted herself. And what poor Norman would have to say if he ever discovered how his cousin had taken advantage of his absence didn't bear thinking about. And what he would think if she ever told him how Luke's kiss had affected her made her mind boggle.

She arrived at Monk's Hall very ruffled. Dozens of cars were parked on the main driveway, spilling out into the quiet street. She spotted the gun-metal Ferrari and clamped her teeth together, groaning as the unwelcome memory of how it had felt to be in his arms stirred stinging sensation to life in her loins.

People were already taking their seats in the long salon. Many of those occupying the folding wooden seats were obviously onlookers, peering round avidly at each newcomer. But Luke Derringer, standing, his elegantly dark-suited back to her as he looked out from one of the tall windows, was no onlooker.

He would, if he could, turn this potentially beautiful home into an expensive hotel, small but prestigious, a means of pouring yet more money into his already heavily laden pockets! He would take it from her if he could, just as he would take kisses on a whim, and, she decided, her face going hot, just as much more as she could be persuaded to 'allow'!

Some men were like that. A fleeting attraction was all it took. And the more unscrupulous among them—such as Luke Derringer—wouldn't turn a hair even if the object of the fleeting, shallow physical attraction happened to be engaged to a member of his own family!

But women were different. They allowed their emotions to become involved, and if they weren't careful could end up betrayed and hurt. But she, Annie, knew how to be careful, to rank a man's character higher than the transient lusts of the flesh. At least, she hoped she did!

She slipped into a vacant seat in the centre of the back row, murmuring her excuses as she edged past an elderly farmer and two stout women with almost identical red faces beneath garish headscarves. Her heartbeat was fast, too fast, and she knew she had to compose herself before the serious business of bidding began.

The woman on her left leaned forward and began gossiping with a faded man in a trilby on the row in front and Annie leaned back, closing her eyes, taking deep, slow breaths. Luke Derringer wouldn't take this house from her, she silently vowed. That he had already taken something more important she wasn't yet ready to admit. But, whatever happened, she wasn't going to let him emerge the victor in this battle for Monk's Hall. She would use every last penny of her father's legacy to ensure it didn't happen.

During her lifetime she'd had precious little to thank her father for. He and her mother had already been divorced by the time she'd reached her first birthday. In all those years she'd never received so much as a postcard from him. But now she sent a private prayer of thankfulness because he had remembered her at the end of his life.

From the head of the room someone called for silence and after a buzz of quickening interest the room became unnaturally quiet as the auctioneer took his place.

After banging his hammer he looked at the sea of faces, announced the reserve price set by the client and went on to extol the virtues of the house, quoting from the catalogue when he said that Monk's Hall had been built in the reign of Queen Anne on the site of an ancient monastery.

As he opened the bidding a gaunt-eyed man whom Annie recognised as one of the local vets raised his catalogue, and the auctioneer nodded.

'I have a bid of one hundred and five thousand, ladies and gentlemen.'

Annie's fingers clenched tightly around her own catalogue, the paper feeling smooth and cool. Normal interest would push the bidding a fair bit higher. She would wait for the faint-hearted to be weeded out.

Carefully, she watched the back of Luke's head, sleek, dark, relaxed. He hadn't made a move. But, like her, he wouldn't join battle just yet. Her heart was pattering wildly as she tried to work out just how much he would be willing to pay. There had to be a certain line beyond which the profitability of the enterprise would become doubtful, she supposed.

The bidding had stuck now with a florid-faced man in the centre of the room, and Annie raised her catalogue.

'Two hundred thousand,' the auctioneer intoned expressionlessly.

From the front of the room Luke drawled, 'And ten.'

From then on the bidding went on relentlessly, with only the two of them in combat. The room was silent save for Annie's cool tones, Luke's drawled responses and the occasional hiss of in-drawn breath from the onlookers as the tension mounted and thickened.

Outwardly calm but inwardly panicking, Annie calculated the amount of her own savings plus the surrender value of her life insurance policy, and made what would have to be her final bid.

For long, agonising moments her breath stuck in her throat, hurting her. Had Norman been here, she thought wildly, pressing the clammy palms of her hands together, then she could have asked him to add a little of his own financial weight.

But he wasn't here, and even if he had been, she acknowledged sickly, he would have been aghast at the amount she had already put on the table. Norman liked a bargain, and at the price Monk's Hall was going to fetch it wasn't one.

The sound of Luke's voice, topping her final bid by yet another ten thousand, came as no real surprise to Annie. In her heart she supposed she had always known that he would emerge the victor in any confrontation between the two of them.

She had lost Monk's Hall and would have to watch as it was turned into an hotel—yet another means of profit for the loathsome Luke Derringer. The blood draining from her face, she sat on her hard wooden seat and hated him as she had never hated anything or anyone in her life.

# CHAPTER THREE

'I'M SORRY about that.' Chris Howard's smooth tones penetrated Annie's raging mind as she tried to slot the key into the car door. She had been the first to walk out of the house, not daring to look to right or left because, if she had, she would have burst into tears. Luke Derringer had stolen the house she'd wanted for herself and Norman. That Norman had finally relented and told her to go ahead and bid had seemed like a good omen. But Luke had come on the scene and spoiled everything.

Chris had stepped into his father's shoes a few years ago, buying up the opposition in the small town, making the old-fashioned, family-owned firm the most successful estate agency and auctioneers in the area.

He looked genuinely concerned as he added, 'I know how you'd set your heart on owning Monk's Hall. Mind you...' his prematurely lined face softened wryly '...even if you'd managed to get it, you'd have had a hell of a job winkling Norman out of his cosy nest on the other side of town!'

She was about to put him straight, to tell him that Norman had already given in, told her to go ahead, even promising to make himself responsible for any structural repairs that needed doing. But Chris was in there before her.

'As a matter of fact, Norman phoned me yesterday. He said you'd be bidding and asked me to look out for you afterwards. He guessed you'd be upset when Derringer walked away with the house you'd wanted and he suggested I take you for coffee. Would you like some? Or something stronger?'

'Why should he do that?' Annie shoved the car key back in her handbag, afraid that her shaky attempts to unlock the door would give her feelings away.

Chris looked embarrassed and that didn't surprise her. She understood what had happened and a new, slower, deeper anger was born. She said tightly, 'Norman only gave me his blessing because he knew I didn't stand a chance against that cousin of his.'

Chris didn't deny it. He looked over her head, his face uncomfortable.

'Giving you false hope was a lousy thing to do. I told him as much. Come on, I'll buy you that coffee.' He took her arm, but she found a smile from somewhere and tugged gently away.

'There's no need, but thank you all the same. There are one or two things I have to do.'

Turning briskly on her heel, she walked away, her back rigid, her footsteps firm and undeviating as she turned on to the narrow, steep walkway that led down beside the grounds of Monk's Hall to the shore.

She needed to be alone to come to terms with what Norman had done, and at this time of the year the beach would probably be deserted. The wide stretch of sand was backed by high unscalable cliffs, the only access from the town itself a narrow road to the small harbour, through the ravine, which was why Seabourne had never grown as a popular tourist resort.

Eventually the path she had taken led down to the narrow road, bordered on one side by the May Brook which rattled its shallow way over stones to debouch into the sea.

She was alone on the windswept ochre sands, and she slipped off her high-heeled shoes, dumping them behind a rock, turned her back on the tiny harbour, and strode towards the foaming water-line.

She had walked for over a mile before she managed to get the worst of her anger under control. For the first time since she had known him she felt respect for Norman withering away. And without their respect for each other, she realised, their relationship was bankrupt.

Had he categorically stated that he was unprepared, ever, to move from The Laurels, then she would naturally have been disappointed but she would have respected his viewpoint, would have accepted it. Where one lived was, after all, less important than with whom one lived.

But he hadn't done that, and he'd only agreed to her putting in a bid when he'd realised his cousin wanted the property. Nor was Luke the type of man to stand aside and allow someone else to take what he wanted. Norman had been well aware of that!

She pushed her fingers through her vivid hair and stood at the water-line, staring out to sea. The water was sparkling, little lights dancing on the tumbling surface, and she sighed, dragging the sharp, clean air into her lungs.

Norman was weak, she acknowledged now. He was content to stand aside and allow Luke to snatch away one of the things she'd wanted most in the world, while letting her believe he was on her side! He had given her hope where he'd known there had been none, and had promptly absented himself so that he wouldn't have to witness her disappointment. He had even asked Chris to look out for her afterwards—so sure had he been that Luke would outbid her!

She wasn't sure if she could ever forgive him for that. So she would face him with it and see how things went from there. She wasn't sure if she could marry him now, spend the rest of her life with a man she couldn't really respect.

Her mouth tightening, she turned and began to walk back, her lips pulling down cynically as she wondered how Norman would react if he discovered that Luke had had ideas of seducing her right under his nose! Would he fight for her, fling his cousin out on his handsome head—or would he simply close his eyes and pretend not to notice?

Not that it would come to that, she reassured herself firmly, as the very thought of being seduced by Luke, under Norman's nose or not, made her feel hot and peculiar. For one thing, she comforted herself, Luke would be leaving, probably today, since there was nothing to keep him here now that Monk's Hall was his. And, for another thing, she wouldn't allow it to happen. She had successfully kept him at bay all week.

Except for this morning, a tiny, unwelcome inner voice reminded her. Except for this morning. And her response to his kiss, to his voice and his wicked hands, hadn't been exactly reassuring from her viewpoint!

So the sooner he left, the better, she conceded honestly, then dragged in her breath because she could see a lone figure walking towards her. Distance in no way diminished that potent male charisma. Horribly, her skin tingled and her heart lurched—and there had to be something very potent indeed about a man who could do that to her at a distance of several hundred yards.

Gritting her teeth, she walked steadily towards him, because there was nowhere else to go unless she turned and ran. And that no man alive could make her do!

He was just standing now, totally relaxed, waiting for her to reach him, the slight breeze from the sea lifting the dark softness of his hair. I'll shoot when I see the whites of his eyes, she thought grimly, because no way would she have allowed him to see how he'd hurt her. He had taken Monk's Hall and she was aching inside.

Still walking steadily, she gathered her mental resources until, still a couple of yards away, she fired her first shot.

'Congratulations. You've acquired a beautiful property.' She carried on walking, not deviating from her path by an inch, and would have passed right by him, a slight smile fixed painfully on her face, but one strong hand lazed out and caught her arm, pulling her to a reluctant and undignified halt. Annie swallowed an unidentifiable lump in her throat and said frigidly, 'Please let me go.'

'In a moment.'

Both hands were holding her now and he might as well have said, 'When I'm good and ready,' because that was what he'd meant. She could read that much in the steady blue glint of his eyes.

Masking her feelings, she glared haughtily back at him. She would have died before she allowed him an inkling of the havoc he was creating inside her. The mere touch of his hands set her on fire. She could feel every one of his finger-ends through the stuff of her suit jacket; the awareness unnerved her.

'Annie . . . I'm sorry about Monk's Hall,' he said softly. If she'd been an idiot she might have believed him, because the hard, sometimes mocking lines of his face had softened to something resembling compassion. But she wasn't an idiot and this man had a thousand faces, all of them devious, and if he thought that a little soft-soaping from him, a spurious regret or two, would get her melting into his arms—and thus round off his stay here nicely— then he had another think coming!

'I know how you'd set your heart on living there with Norman, but don't you see——' his fingers tightened fractionally as he drew her closer to him '—it would never have worked? I've known him all my life, on and off, and he hasn't changed. He likes his comforts and he likes them to be functional.

He'd have been out of his depth, rattling around Monk's Hall.'

'Are you trying to tell me that you bought that place—and paid way over the odds for it, too—merely to save Norman from a horrid fate?' she said grittily, emphasising her scorn with a look that would have withered any man but Luke Derringer.

'No, I didn't say that.'

His air of patience was galling, raising her temperature, and she growled, 'Then save your sympathy; it's not needed. You beat me over the house, but it's not the end of the world.'

'No?' His eyes softened with a misty pity that made her spitting mad. She didn't want anyone's pity, least of all his. 'Then why the long solitary walk?' he questioned astutely. 'You had too many things to do to have lunch with me, so why the sudden urge for time-wasting solitude? I saw you from the grounds of the Hall. I knew you had to be hurting. I came to sympathise.'

'How gracious!' Annie snapped her teeth at him, her eyes dark with a fury she feared she would not be able to contain much longer. She jerked her arms, but his grasp was unwavering. 'Didn't it occur to your monstrous ego that I would make any excuse to get out of spending time with you? Now let me go!'

'Of course.' To her secret amazement he released her arms, his eyes suddenly bleak.

Amazement? she questioned a reeling brain as she strode away as quickly as her narrow skirt would permit. Regret might have been nearer the mark, she decided with an honesty that had her near to loathing herself. She had fully—and not without a strange, wild inner excitement—expected him to repeat the kiss of this morning!

He was an opportunist of the most selfish kind, and the fact that he had simply released her without taking what he had openly admitted he wanted was totally out of character.

But they were both behaving out of character, she admitted wryly. It wasn't her nature to allow casual sexual excitement to take over. She had more respect for her body than that. Not that it had taken over, of course. Not yet, a small inner voice said snidely. Not yet.

Finding the rock where she had left her shoes, she stuffed her feet into them and only then permitted herself to look round. Luke was not following her, as she had apprehensively anticipated, but was moving away down the beach, his easy stride taking him far away.

Hopefully, that would be the last she would see of him, she thought with weak relief. This afternoon she would be taking herself off for what remained of the weekend. She needed time to calm down before she tackled Norman over the way he had so sneakily manipulated her over Monk's Hall. Their whole future together was on the line, and she had to think sensibly, to get things into perspective, before she tossed it aside in a moment of anger.

\* \* \*

'Where on earth have you been?' Joan shot out of
the front door as Annie parked the runabout. 'The
auction was over hours ago!'

Reluctant to face Norman while she was still in
an evil mood, Annie had taken her time. She had
driven into town and phoned Cassie from a call-
box. Her friendship with Cassandra Wilkes went
back years. They had shared a couple of rooms in
Clerkenwell while Annie had been at secretarial
college.

At nearly eighteen Annie had plucked up the
courage to tell her mother that she was leaving,
striking out on her own. She had been tired of the
enforced role of number one fan and ego-booster,
of being carted around from one glitzy hotel to
another, rarely staying anywhere longer than it took
for a film to be shot or a play to complete its run.
Tired of being pushed into the background because
she had suddenly developed a beauty of her own
and Willa Kennedy didn't like to have beautiful
women around her—and that included her own
daughter.

At that time Annie's new-found independence
had been a bit scary, her veneer of self-confidence
wafer-thin. And Cassie, older by four years, had
been just the sort of friend she had needed. Cassie
still worked and lived in London, now having an
apartment in Chelsea, where Annie knew she was
always welcome.

But when she got through to her friend on the
phone, Cassie had said, her voice distorted by static
on the line, 'Come by all means. Only I'm off on

holiday—you only just caught me. But if you want a day or two in town you're welcome. I'll leave the key with the guy downstairs, but next time, buster, make sure you come when I can enjoy your company!'

Annie had been disappointed at first, but soon realised that it might be better to spend the short time available on her own. Together, she and Cassie tended to sit up half the night, giggling and gossiping and catching up on all the news. Time was short: Annie needed to be back in Seabourne on Monday morning when she and Norman were due to spend a couple of days interviewing Professor Rhys and taking the photographs needed to illustrate that section of the book.

Aware now that Joan was regarding her with cold impatience, Annie walked reluctantly towards the bungalow. She would simply tell Norman she fancied a day in town—no need to tell him that Cassie would be away, and that she'd be spending the time trying to decide if marrying him was the right thing to do. Until today she'd had no significant doubts at all.

'You certainly know when to make yourself scarce!' Joan's mouth was a disapproving slash, but her eyes were glittering with something that looked remarkably like excitement. She made no move to let Annie pass; it was almost as if the older woman were barring the way, refusing to let her over the threshold.

'Why, have I missed something?' Annie spoke tartly, in no mood at the moment for Joan's antics.

Ever since she and Norman had become engaged she had worried over Joan's suddenly antagonistic behaviour. Now she had far more important things to occupy her mind and she said, 'Excuse me, Joan,' trying to walk past the housekeeper's solid figure, but stopped in her tracks when Joan answered, sounding almost triumphant,

'There's been an accident.'

'Norman?' Annie's face went pale, the faint scattering of freckles across the bridge of her nose standing out starkly. 'What happened?'

She had spent the afternoon grumbling at him in her mind—when she hadn't been mentally occupied with Luke! And all the time he had been...?

'He hurt his back.' Joan folded her arms in front of her, standing her ground. 'We came back from shopping and while I was washing up after lunch he went in the garden. The next thing I knew he was calling for me. He'd tried to move the garden seat and cricked his back. Dr Beddowes doesn't think it's a disc, but he's ordered him to bed, flat on his back for the duration. It's been all go, I can tell you.'

'It must have been,' Annie agreed drily, relieved that it was nothing worse. She pushed past Joan, but the housekeeper's voice stopped her.

'I wouldn't disturb him if I were you. He's asleep. After I'd called the doctor out, and he'd examined him, I managed to get him to bed. The poor soul was in agony, couldn't even bend to take his own shoes and socks off!' Her grey eyes taunted, but Annie shrugged coolly.

'I'm sure you made him as comfortable as possible. Thank you.'

Joan nodded, her posture important. 'If you want something to eat, there's some salad. Help yourself—I'm going to unearth the sunray lamp, and I sent Luke to the chemist for something for me to rub on Norman's back.'

She bustled away, and Annie thought, You'll enjoy rubbing his back, won't you? And fussing around him and making yourself indispensable. And she was more than ever sure that she'd been right in thinking that Joan had been in love with Norman for years and that jealousy had turned a kindly, cheerful woman into a shrew.

And why was Luke still hanging around? She had imagined he'd be eager to get out of this one-horse town to hand the planning and development details of Monk's Hall over to his hirelings. She wondered if he'd bother to say goodbye before he finally left, and hoped he wouldn't. Even so, there was a stupid ache just beneath her breastbone at the thought of never actually seeing him again.

Her perverse thoughts both surprised and dismayed her. Her fiancé was lying in bed, probably in pain, and she had carelessly handed his care over to Joan, without one qualm, and had immediately turned her entire attention to the hateful Luke. There had to be something very wrong with her!

Perplexed by her own contrary attitude, and determined to do something about it, she went to her room to comb the tangles out of her hair before looking in on Norman. She decided she wouldn't

mention Monk's Hall until later, until he was over
the shock of being confined to bed, and she would
sympathise with him over his accident, because she
owed him that, at least. And then she would have
to cancel the interviews with Professor Rhys, and
she wouldn't avail herself of Cassie's flat because
she could do whatever thinking she had to do here.

She was calmer now, and her initial fear that
Norman's accident had been something far worse
than a cricked back had brought home to her just
how fond of him she was.

They were fond of each other, but was fondness
enough? She caught sight of her reflected frown
and sighed. She simply didn't know any more. And
she had been so sure. They had both agreed that
passionate love had no place in their lives, and that
a marriage based on mutual fondness and respect,
on compatible interests, on a normal need for companionship and children—when Annie felt ready
for motherhood—was far more sensible than a
union based on the transitory lusts of the flesh.

Norman's biggest regret was that his first wife
hadn't been able to give him children, and Annie
wanted a family of her own to love. But was
Norman the right father for her children?

The doubts simply wouldn't go away. Did she
really want to spend the rest of her life with
Norman? Or would she always be looking for
strengths in him she now knew he didn't possess?
And would even the simplest display of honest-to-
goodness emotion be forever taboo?

*    *    *

Norman was lying flat on his back, looking sorry for himself.

'I'm sorry you lost Monk's Hall,' he said.

Despite her good intentions, Annie bit out tersely, 'Are you? Are you really?' Then she tacked on sincerely, 'And I'm sorry about your back. Does it hurt?'

'If I try to move, yes. According to Beddowes, I've wrenched some muscles and the only cure is lying here.'

He had dismissed her questioning of the veracity of his statement over her loss of Monk's Hall, she noted drily, as she pulled up a chair. He had a talent for ignoring what he didn't want to see or hear. Only now was she beginning to realise how self-centred he was. And this was the room she would share with him if they married. It depressed her utterly. But now wasn't the time to think about future colour schemes, about replacing the heavy, ugly nineteen-forties furniture with something else. She said optimistically, 'Perhaps it will only take a day or two.'

But Norman grumbled, 'Beddowes mentioned four to six weeks. If you'd been around we would have moved that seat together and this wouldn't have happened. Where were you?'

Wondering if we ought to call the marriage off, Annie thought, but she said, 'You should have waited. That seat's heavy—it could have been shifted any time.'

'I distinctly remember asking you to help me with it this afternoon.'

And she thought, And I distinctly remember thinking there'd be no need because we wouldn't be living here much longer. But you knew better, didn't you? You knew Luke would outbid me.

If Norman hadn't been in pain nothing would have stopped her from speaking her thoughts out loud. As it was, she merely said, 'I'll phone Professor Rhys and cancel our visit,' and brought a hornets' nest around her ears.

'You can't do that!' Norman snapped, struggling to rise but falling back on the mattress with a yowl of pain. 'It will be weeks before I'm fit to go. I can't afford to waste that amount of time.' Annoyed, he showed a purple face and Annie stared at him as if seeing him for the first time. He had never had occasion to be anything other than pleased with her before now. 'You must go on your own,' he told her firmly. 'You know what I'm looking for. The book was your idea in the first place.'

'Well, I would, but——'

'No buts, please. Joan can look after me perfectly well, if that's what's worrying you.'

It wasn't. And Joan would like nothing better than to look after him for the rest of his life. Annie opened her mouth to explain her problem, but Norman shot at her accusingly, 'In fact, she's been a marvel. I don't know what I'd have done without her this afternoon. And when you get back from Wales we can go through the notes together, make a start on the relevant chapter.'

His blunt features looked pinched with the discomfort he was experiencing. She knew how important his work was to him, and she was his research assistant, after all, but she could see a problem.

'What about the photographs? I can't handle the Hasselblad.' It was a piece of beautiful, professional equipment, technically highly complex, and she didn't begin to know how to use it. Give her a simple camera, where everything was automatic, foolproof, and she'd still probably manage to point the thing in the wrong direction!

'For pity's sake, woman!'

Annie had never heard Norman bellow before; he was obviously fed up with everything, herself included, and Luke chose that moment to enter the room, his smile easy, his husky voice holding slightly cynical undertones as he asked, 'Lovers' tiff?' He put a tube of ointment on the bedside table and glanced from Norman's petulant scowl to Annie's set features. 'Anything wrong?' He spoke mildly, as if addressing two squabbling children.

Norman muttered sarcastically, 'Not so as you'd notice. I'm stuck here for weeks and my research assistant——' he glared at Annie with disgust '—is refusing to interview Professor Rhys because she's afraid of using a simple piece of photographic equipment. The fact that I need to get this information is of no consequence, it would appear.'

Annie would have stalked out of the room at this point. He was making her sound like a selfish idiot and, in any case, she didn't want the subject of their

quarrel to be discussed with the objectionable Luke.
Norman was beginning to irritate her beyond endurance, but something—pride, she thought—held
her where she was, had her explaining stiltedly, 'I
am not refusing to do anything. I merely pointed
out that the workings of the Hasselblad are a
mystery to me. I am perfectly willing to interview
Professor Rhys, but——'

'Well, in that case, you can both relax. Your
problems are solved.' Luke rocked back on his
heels, his hands negligently thrust into the pockets
of his tight-fitting jeans, and Annie had to drag her
eyes away from the way the dark blue material
moulded the male power of his thighs.

He had changed his clothes since this morning,
she noted sourly, his casual gear making him look
even more dangerous, if that were possible. And
she closed her eyes in hopeless resignation, grinding
her teeth because her intuition—so finely tuned
where this one man was concerned—told her exactly
what was coming next. And huskily, lazily, he
drawled the very words she'd been afraid of
hearing.

'I'll go in your place, Norman. Annie can look
after the interviews, of course, but I'll do the pho-
tography. I can handle your camera. No problem.'

Painfully, she wrenched her eyes open, feeling
her heart lurch and bump around beneath her
breastbone. Norman was making grateful clucking
noises, but she wasn't listening to him. She was
watching Luke's eyes. Deep, dark blue depths she
could feel herself drowning in. And she was mind-

lessly absorbing the silent, mocking message those eyes were transmitting, a message that her terrified brain translated as, And I can handle your fiancée, too. No problem. No problem at all!

# CHAPTER FOUR

'NERVOUS, Annie?' Luke's voice drifted over her, lazy and intimate, filling the luxurious confines of the racy car, threading her pulsebeats with dread. He was easy on the ear, easy on the eye, and could, if she let him, be easy on the senses. Oh, so easy.

'Should I be? I'm not unused to handling interviews. I am Norman's research assistant.' Deliberately she misunderstood him. He was not referring to the coming interviews. His question had been loaded with meaning, making her instantly and painfully aware of the compulsive and, on her part, highly unwelcome attraction there was between them.

'You probably should be nervous,' he admitted softly. 'You know exactly why I offered to come along on this trip.'

That was an unequivocal statement, but one she was going to twist around if she could. She watched with unwilling fascination as his strongly made yet elegant hands lightly gripped the steering wheel, and said, a shade too sweetly, 'To help poor Norman out. What else?'

'You're quite wrong.' He took his remarkable eyes from the road for a second, and the smile he gave her was intimate and knowing, shocking in its wickedness.

Her reactions to this man had been shocking her ever since she'd first set eyes on him and her insides churned around sickeningly as he told her, 'I offered because I wanted to be with you. We have a lot to say to each other—though you probably won't allow yourself to admit it. And Norman's quite capable of looking after himself. All he ever needs to do is sit back and put on his helpless academic look to have everyone around him rushing to make his life easy. It's a knack he has. He gets what he wants from life by being passive.'

'While you take the opposite course,' she couldn't help snapping. 'You actively go out and grab!'

'You could be right, at that.' Humour warmed his voice. He was impervious. Nothing she could say or do riled him, shook that monumental self-assurance of his. But his answer scared her; he was admitting his inborn, driving need actively to take what he wanted. And for some reason he wanted her. He had said so. And she, dammit, despite her principles, could so easily be taken. The shaming knowledge worried her, more than anything had ever worried her before; she felt she no longer really knew herself.

She turned her head sharply, forbidding herself the sight of that aggressive profile, the strong hands on the wheel, the too-close muscular thighs lovingly moulded by dark blue denim. Stoically, she clamped her eyes on the passing scenery, clamped her soft lips together lest their quivering alert him to precisely how his nearness affected her.

'You warned the Prof I'd be arriving in Norman's place?'

His voice was an intrusion, the question unwelcome because it needed an answer. She muttered, 'Yes, of course,' and stared fixedly through the window.

The mountains were higher now, more barren. The narrow, twisting ribbon of road snaked through the rugged pass but the powerful Ferrari treated the devilish gradients with contempt. Like its owner, she thought grumpily. Luke Derringer would take all life's obstacles in his effortless stride, mastering them with that damnably smooth self-confidence of his. Norman had told her, a hint of green in his voice, that Luke had made his first clear million before he was twenty-five. Astute buying in the hotel property market, transforming rundown near slums to classy five-star affairs which appealed to those who didn't know the meaning of a budget, had set him well on his way, and he'd been travelling upwards ever since. Single-mindedness and determination were gifts in his capable hands, gifts to be used. And if he chose to apply them to his terrifying pursuit of herself, then what chance did she have? She shuddered.

'So? Did he mind?' asked Luke, with a warning edge to his voice which eased off a touch as he added, 'You might like to know I've got ways of treating a sulky woman.'

'I'm shaking in my shoes!' she snapped right back. She wasn't sulking, merely allowing her instinct for self-preservation its head! The less she

had to do with this man, the better, and that included normal civilised conversation! But she told
him resignedly, 'He didn't mind at all. He was just
thankful the interviews hadn't been cancelled. From
what I could gather, he gets lonely. His home—
Plas-y-draig—is pretty remote. The nearest inn's
eight miles away and pretty basic, he tells me.'

'So that's why we're staying with him? I had
wondered,' Luke commented, and Annie nodded.

'He suggested it when I arranged the interviews
in the first place. It would save time, he said, and
he'd be glad of the company.'

She didn't add that Professor Rhys had told her,
when she'd phoned to explain that Luke would be
taking Norman's place, that he had his young
grandson staying with him at present. Let that, and
her secret intention to spend as much time as possible in the company of either the lonely old man or
his young grandson, come as one big surprise!

Pointing Luke and the Hasselblad right out of
the way while she stuck to the Professor like a
limpet would give her great satisfaction. Never, if
she could help it, would she be alone with Luke.
He would soon discover that, despite his avowed
intention to have her to himself, she was quite
capable of thwarting him at every turn.

The thought amused her and she relaxed her tense
shoulders slightly, only to find her whole body vir-
tually seize up as Luke turned the car on to a grav-
elled stopping-place at the side of the lonely road.

'What are you doing?' Suspicion laced her voice,
made it unnaturally sharp.

Luke's response was grim. 'Planning a major seduction scene, what else? Would you believe me if I said we'd run out of petrol?'

She could tell her edginess was beginning to really annoy him and was glad. Why should she be the only one to have her teeth regularly set on edge?

'I would expect you to show more originality than that,' she told him huffily, then wondered why she felt so relieved when his features lightened with an appreciative smile.

'You're learning!' he murmured.

He slewed round in his seat, taking the keys from the ignition, dangling them lightly between his fingers, his deep eyes following the contours of her face, her body—clad in a snug-fitting apple-green tracksuit.

Appalled, she felt her skin tingle, running with heat where his eyes touched her, and a hot stab of naked desire wreaked its havoc deep within her. She blushed, shamed by her body's treachery.

'The truth is that I had Joan fix us a picnic lunch.' His words were prosaic enough, but his eyes told her he had noted that betraying blush, knew the reason for it, too. 'I thought we might eat it here— if we can't find anything more interesting to do,' he told her, his eyes glinting wickedly.

Blushing again, and furious with herself because of it, she scrambled out of the car and stumbled over the gravel. He was a sneaky bastard, an egocentric sex maniac, and she was a fool for letting him affect her the way he did!

Her lips compressed, she stared at the view. From the stone parapet at the edge of the stopover the scenery was breathtaking—or would have been if her breath hadn't already been well and truly taken by that ravening wolf back there! But as Luke fetched the hamper she forced herself to concentrate on the view, and only on that.

Beneath the pale crisp blue of the arching autumn sky the valley below was picked out in shades of gold and silver. A stone farmhouse, as small from there as a child's toy, snuggled against a background of golden-leafed trees, the foaming stream that wound its shallow way along the valley floor a thread of silver. Above her, a hawk drifted, deceptively graceful and lazy but intrinsically predatory, and suddenly, at her side, was the man—just as predatory, his lazy grace a cloak that concealed deadly purpose.

Annie shivered convulsively and he lifted one eyebrow. 'Cold? Surely not.' He cupped an unwelcome hand beneath her elbow, making her veins run with fire. 'We'll eat over there.'

Using his own brand of velvet domination, he guided her through a narrow aperture at the side of the stone safety wall. She was going along with him because she had little choice, she told herself. She might be pliable in small things, she meted out reassurances to herself like a necessary drug, but not in the big things, the things that really mattered. Things like not allowing Luke to seduce her senses when she was engaged to his cousin! And in any case, she couldn't really be attracted to a man who would behave so dishonourably, could she?

So why did her entire body seem to melt, to dissolve into absurd insubstantiality when he slid an arm around her waist, his hand pressing into the soft, womanly swell of her hips as he pulled her close to the hard, lean length of him while they negotiated the narrow track?

At the base of the track a relatively level space of ground offered a place for a picnic. A place for whatever else he intended, she thought, shuddering. Plonking herself as far away from him as she could get without falling off the mountain, Annie cupped her chin in her hands, her big brown eyes fixed on the brooding mass of mountains on the other side of the valley.

Beneath her the short thin grass was crisp and carried the scent of sun-warmed rock, of living, breathing mountainside, and, in the distance, she could hear the chuckle of shallow water, the liquid note of a bird. And she wondered if she would have been so aware, so clearly aware of herself, of her surroundings, if Norman had been with her, not Luke. And knew, to her mortification, that she would not.

She barely touched the slice of quiche Luke handed her on a paper plate, and merely nibbled at the fresh tomato, its skin warm, its flesh cool and tangy. But she drained the beaker of strong hot coffee as if it might save her life.

Breaking the silence he had maintained since they had come to this secluded place, Luke remarked,

'So your mother's a celebrated actress? I knew Willa Kennedy had had several husbands, but I didn't know she had a daughter.'

Not many people did. Her mother's various marriages had been widely publicised, but her daughter had been kept well in the background. Annie didn't particularly want to talk about her mother, to think about the seventeen years spent trailing in her wake like some insignificant pebble attached to the glittering train of a shooting star. That was all in the past and, to Annie, looking back wasn't particularly productive.

She lifted one shoulder dismissively. 'Who told you?'

'Norman, of course. He also said he'd never met her.'

And that wasn't because Norman hadn't been eager to meet the world-famous actress, Annie thought drearily, but she had wanted to prepare Norman for the star's inevitable reaction to a future son-in-law. Trouble was, Norman didn't have a sense of humour. And one needed to see the funny side of Willa Kennedy in order to swallow her wiles. Because whenever a member of the male sex had shown an interest in Annie Willa had promptly snatched him away, drawn him into her own glitzy orbit, keeping him there for as long as it pleased her to do so.

It hadn't mattered; Annie had been able to handle it with a philosophical attitude rare in one of her tender years. Until Hernando Carreras had hap-

pened along in the summer when she was seventeen
and then it had been different, very different . . .

'And apparently you only wrote and told your
mother of your engagement a couple of weeks ago,
and that at Norman's insistence.' The husky voice
prodded her.

Bright as a button, hiding her annoyance at his
probing into what was none of his business, Annie
clipped out, 'So? Willa's a busy woman, and up
until a couple of weeks ago she'd been totally absorbed in the new film she was making. Family demands only break her concentration.' And the news
that her daughter was engaged would make her
restless, restless enough to make one of her dra-
matic entrances, seeing the fact of a man in little
Annie's life as a challenge that couldn't be resisted.

Luke was repacking the hamper, as she could hear
from the rustle of foil, the clatter of beakers, the
final snap as the clasp was closed. And now was
the time to get to her feet, lob a smile vaguely in
his direction and say that it was time they were
moving because the Professor would be thinking
they were lost.

But she didn't move. She was held immobile by
his eyes. The way Luke made her so aware of
herself, of him, was beginning to terrify her.

She regretted her lack of movement, of direction,
as soon as she felt the light feathering of his fingertips on the soft nape of her neck, just beneath the
glossy strands of her hair. One touch was all it
needed to make her shockingly aware of his mas-
culinity, aware as never before of her own femi-

ninity, of the inevitability of the sexual equation. One touch, that was all.

'Did Willa hurt you badly?'

An unsuspected tenderness in his voice devastated her, made her want to cry. But she had shed all the tears she was ever going to shed over Willa years ago. Besides, she didn't want this sort of closeness, not with him. He was too shallow, his needs, where she was concerned, too transitory. She said stonily, 'Of course not, Willa spoilt me rotten.' And that wasn't too far from the truth. If a good mood had coincided with her remembering she had a daughter, her mother had been known to shower her with wildly expensive and totally inappropriate gifts.

'Is that so?' His tone was soothing but faintly sceptical, and his fingers stroked, smooth warm fingers intent on discovering the delicate contours of her nape, her throat. Sliding, seductive fingers insidiously awakening something too long dormant, something she had tried to suppress.

She muttered, 'Don't,' croakily. She felt curiously weak, incapable of movement...

Luke ignored her uselessly half-hearted protest, moving his hard body closer so that, sitting more behind than beside her, he seemed to be cradling her, his big body both protective and demanding, and all male, very much so.

She shuddered, pulling a ragged breath through flaring nostrils as his persuasive fingers splayed at the base of her throat, sliding easily, too easily, beneath the loose collar of her tracksuit top.

'No!' she muttered hoarsely as his hand unerr-
ingly cupped one firm, rounded breast, and 'No!'
again as her treacherous flesh hardened, pressing
an umistakable invitation against the bone-melting
warmth of his palm.

But 'Yes, oh, yes,' Luke murmured throatily,
dragging her round in his arms, and his vivid eyes
held hers for one splinter of time, their message
quite readable, quite terrifying, before his dark head
came down and she closed her eyes, blotting out
everything but the sensation, the devilish assault of
his kiss.

It went deep, that kiss, making her mindless. She
could feel the heavy thud of his heart against the
wild pattering of her own as he made a luxury of
his now lingering exploration of the sweet recesses
of her mouth. And she felt his body shudder, transmitting messages that were painfully sweet, and was
hardly aware of the way her hands twisted in the
cool, crisp darkness of his hair, her fingertips
finding the warmth of his skull.

The citadel of her body was shaking on its foun-
dations ... Only one man had made the earth move
for her before, and she had vowed that she would
be very sure of her man before she allowed it to
happen again ...

Wrenching away from him took all her moral
courage. She scrambled to her feet, shaking, her
body hurting with fiercely denied need, her eyes
feverish, defiant.

'Just keep your vile hands off me!' she flung
breathlessly, disgust with herself more painful than

her disgust with him. He was an opportunist, a man on the make, while she was a woman who had vowed never to pander to sexuality, never to indulge in casual lovemaking. She had chosen the safer, the more sensible path, with her eyes wide open. Very wide open, seeing both sides of the picture and making her choice.

But lithely he was on his feet, too, right beside her,

'You don't mean that,' he bit out tersely, ice-cold lights glinting in the depths of his clever eyes. 'You know damned well exactly how it's been between us ever since we met.'

So she did, she acknowledged hollowly, the uncomfortable thought drilling away at her mind. She had recognised the instantaneous reaction, one to the other, the dark, primeval force of feeling that electrified the very air surrounding them, need calling to need in a cry as old and pagan as time.

She might hear that call, loud and clear, but she wasn't answering, not when it came from the type of man who would seduce his own cousin's fiancée without one single qualm! Seduce her, and then, as was his custom, move on to the next easy conquest. No way—she had too much respect for herself to allow that to happen!

Grimly, she brushed clinging particles of grass from her apple-green pants, her features set in lines as cold and precise as any created by a mason from a block of stone.

Luke said rawly, 'I want to take you to bed,' and her heart kicked beneath her breastbone, her thighs turning to liquid fire at the mind-pictures that statement presented.

But, above the thundering of her blood she heard her own voice clipping thinly, 'Why? So that you can scurry back to Norman, boasting of how you seduced me?'

'Why should I do that?' There was a strange glitter in his eyes and his mouth was hard, cynical.

'Because you'd hardly known me for five minutes before you were accusing me of marrying him for financial security,' she reminded him acidly. 'They say blood's thicker than water, so it might make you feel good to protect your cousin from a gold-digger!'

She picked up the hamper and was walking away from him, her sneaker-clad feet slapping the ground as if she would imprint the flinty subsoil with her determination.

'Not financial security,' he corrected, following her, his big body a handspan away, making her want to scream. 'Norman already told me you'd in-herited a packet from your father.'

They had reached the car now and she faced him. There was nowhere else to go.

'And what else has he told you about me?' she growled, stung by the revelation. How much more of her personal affairs had Norman divulged to Luke? She hadn't imagined him as being disloyal, a tattler; she was beginning to feel she didn't know him at all.

PASSIONATE AWAKENING73

'Enough.' He took the hamper from her and tossed it carelessly into the back of the car. 'Enough to tell me that he's no more in love with you than you are with him.' His eyes narrowed, impaling her with glittering intensity, the soft huskiness of his voice a devilish contrast that totally unnerved her. 'There are other kinds of security, Annie. With Norman it's a need to be pampered and comfortable, to know that the best research assistant he's ever likely to have—and one, moreover, who won't be a financial or emotional drain on him— is willing to stick around and make him nice and cosy until death do you part. And you, Annie, what is it with you?'

He moved closer, slowly, and the fierce chemical reaction there was between them kept her where she was, her eyes riveted on the tangle of dark body hair against the bronzed satin skin revealed by the open-necked shirt he wore.

'You use Norman like a security blanket because you're afraid of something. Not of financial hardship—we've proved that. And not because you're afraid of being left on the shelf—you're too damned attractive for that prospect to worry you. So what is it?'

His voice had deepened, the lines of his mouth softening as he lifted her small rounded chin with the tip of one finger, probing blue irises meeting wary brown.

'Not telling, hmm?' The slow, easy huskiness of his voice raised goosebumps on her burning flesh.

'Not to worry.' His lips brushed hers lightly, teasingly, before he turned away to unlock the car door. 'I fully intend to find out—and that's something I'm going to enjoy.'

# CHAPTER FIVE

WITH the sounds of that threat echoing through her brain Annie retained a stiff, ungiving silence for the remainder of the journey, and Luke, thankfully, seemed lost in thoughts of his own.

He had arbitrarily decided that she and Norman didn't love each other, had openly admitted he wanted her in his bed, and had talked about getting to know what made her tick as if the exercise would be an amusing game. Well, she was a person in her own right, wasn't she? Not some pliable, doll-brained creature fashioned for his temporary sexual gratification. Her body, her emotions, were not his to be used simply because, for the moment, he fancied her! And the sooner she made him understand she wasn't about to fall into his arms and into his bed, the better!

She gave a sudden, decisive snort and turned her attention to the view. The afternoon sky had become overcast and the mountains brooded, stark and ancient on either side of the narrow track they had taken, the cloud shapes, gathering and thickening, darkened the wild landscape.

It had begun to rain as they'd passed through the huddled village of Bryn-y-draig, and it had turned into a deluge by the time they turned off the narrow mountain road between two stone pillars, both of which had the name Plas-y-draig carved into their sides.

Thank heavens, Annie thought. She couldn't stand much more of this stinging silence. The shaming memory of the way he'd kissed her, of the things he'd said, made her brain ache.

The grey stone house itself was of such dour and Gothic proportions—complete with turrets and mock battlements—that under any other circumstances Annie would have laughed aloud. As it was, she could only think of getting herself inside the monstrosity and sticking to Professor Rhys for protection!

Protection more from herself than from the silent man at her side, she admitted in a mood of self-disgust. He had said, with an audacity only he was capable of, that he wanted her in his bed but, whatever his faults—and they were legion as far as she was concerned—he wouldn't stoop to rape. If she found herself in his bed it would be because she had gone there willingly. And with the memories of how it had felt to be in his arms still making her skin quiver she knew she could easily find herself in that humiliating and degrading situation if she weren't very careful!

'Go wake the Professor up,' Luke instructed as he switched off the ignition. 'I'll bring the bags. There's no sense in both of us getting soaked.'

He had drawn the Ferrari up behind a rusty Mini and the rain was coming down in thick silver sheets now, shrouding everything but the façade of the wet grey house and the encroaching giant rhododendrons from view. Annie nodded, her smile grim, wondering if a thorough soaking would dampen his damned ardour, then scuttled through the deluge to the relative shelter of the massive porch.

The heavy door was dragged open before she had time to knock and a wiry, elderly woman, who was holding a sleepy-eyed small boy in her arms, said, 'Thank heaven you've come. Miss Ross, isn't it?'

Annie nodded, stepping inside as the woman held the door wider. She had button-black eyes in a monkeyish face and looked about at the end of her tether.

Luke had come in by now, carrying the gear and shaking his head like a big dog coming out of water. The monkey-faced woman tutted. 'Such weather! It's all we need on top of everything else! I'm so sorry——'

'Sorry about what, Mrs...?' Luke's gravelly voice was warm, assured, and the elderly woman visibly relaxed. She stopped twittering and shifted the child from one bony hip to the other, smiling now as if encountering Luke had made her day.

'Morgan,' she supplied. 'I come in to do for the Professor once a week. Today's my day, and that's a blessing if ever there was one. I found him collapsed——' She lowered her voice, glancing down at the child, aged about three, who was now sucking his thumb as dark lashes fanned his tear-streaked cheeks. 'I thought the old man had snuffed it—and this poor mite was sobbing his heart out.'

She seemed set to continue in this macabre vein for hours and Annie gave Luke an instinctive glance of sheer gratitude as he took over the situation with gentle but firm authority.

'What has happened, precisely, Mrs Morgan? Where is Professor Rhys now?'

'In hospital, in Aber,' Mrs Morgan told him. 'He's in intensive care. And I don't know what to do for the best. What with you and Miss Ross due to arrive and my Bethan expecting her third any minute, and me having to get over to Llangurig because I promised to look after the other two and Davy—he's her husband—and them with no way of knowing what's held me up...' She shifted the sleepy child again as if he had become an intolerable burden, and Luke wordlessly held out his arms, taking the child, tucking the dark curly head comfortably against his shoulder.

Annie said weakly, concern for the Professor creasing her brow, 'Where are the child's parents?'

'In Canada,' came the doleful reply. 'And his name's Jamie, poor little scrap, and I can't think who will see to him, or what my Bethan will be thinking with me being already two hours late, and her not on the phone, and——'

'Mrs Morgan.' Luke's voice was deeply authoritative, despite its soothing tone, and Annie could only admire the way he went on to elicit the necessary facts: that Jamie's parents, on a short visit to his father's people in Toronto, had already been contacted by the local doctor, and that Jamie's mother, the Professor's daughter, was on standby, waiting for a flight to Birmingham International.

The trouble was, Annie realised, she didn't want to have to admire anything about him, and she was certainly deeply suspicious of a dangerous softening in her which had been brought about by the way he cradled the now sleeping child so protectively in his strong, comforting arms.

Suddenly, she felt achingly cold. The lofty hall was gloomy in the dull half-light, the pelting rain a violent onslaught against the high, rather lurid stained-glass windows.

The news that had greeted them couldn't have been much worse, and her heart went out to the lonely old man who, even now, was fighting for his life.

As if sensing the bleakness of her thoughts, Luke moved closer, his body heat warming her even as it warmed and comforted the sleeping child, the power of his vibrant personality calming her, enfolding her. Briefly, almost gratefully, Annie relinquished herself to his sheer male dominance, listening mutely as he spoke again to Mrs Morgan.

'You've handled everything wonderfully, but there's nothing more you can do here now. You have enough on your plate as it is, so why don't you get over to your daughter's home before they send out a search party? Miss Ross and I will look after Jamie until his mother gets here.'

Mrs Morgan was already pulling on a shabby green raincoat, needing no second telling. 'If you're sure you can manage?' She knotted a headscarf under her chin. 'I feel bad about leaving the little

boy, he's bound to be upset when he finds himself
with strangers, but what else can I do?'

'Nothing, nothing at all. You've done all you
could,' Luke told her, handing Jamie over to Annie
before ushering Mrs Morgan out as she began hur-
riedly trying to tell him where everything was kept,
what Jamie was to have for his tea.

Annie, the child's chubby legs clasped around her
slender body, the weight of his head pressed into
her shoulder, felt her heart contract with an almost
painful surge of protectiveness. She had never held
a child before, and the depth of feeling that simple,
natural act produced astounded her.

Above the lash of the rain she heard the Mini's
engine splutter to life and Luke closed the door,
leaning against it, his face wry.

'There goes one very relieved lady—even if she
does have a conscience about leaving without
showing us where every last cup and saucer can be
found!'

Annie stared at him, her eyes wide. She wanted
to say something innocuous, to defuse the situation
but her throat felt thick, constricted. In closing the
door on the departing Mrs Morgan, on the in-
clement weather, he had isolated them here together,
making the house a prison, forcing them into a
proximity she suddenly feared more than she had
ever feared anything before.

He moved slowly away from the door, his
expression unreadable as he walked over to a large,
heavy table which carried a telephone, with a couple
of directories.

'Why don't you scout around and find the kitchen, make a pot of tea? I'll contact the hospital. Then we'll decide where we are to sleep.'

The way he said that, the husky, intimate quality of his voice, brought a flush to her face and she turned quickly, hiding it, pattering away down a dim corridor, trying doors until she found the kitchen.

It was warmer in here but she was still shuddering with reaction. If he thought she was sleeping with him then he'd have to think again! She hadn't forgotten the way he'd stated, so matter-of-factly, 'I want to take you to bed', and she could still feel the strange inner trembling sensation those terrifying words had produced, still hear his lazily confident voice rattling around inside her head.

Her agitation must have transmitted itself to Jamie because she felt him stir and waken, beginning to wriggle in her arms. Feeling for the switch, she flicked the light on and, immediately, shadowy shapes became solid everyday objects, comfortable and reassuring. A large Aga range was the source of heat and there were pine dressers, a fridge, rocking-chairs with bright patchwork cushions.

Sitting the squirming child on the central scrubbed-pine table she said calmly, smiling, 'Hello, Jamie—I'm Annie and I'm here to look after you until your mother comes home.' She held her breath as he subjected her to a wary stare.

'Grandad,' he uttered, his voice surprisingly gruff, wriggling to get down from the table. But

Annie held him firmly, a hand on either side of his solid body, clad in shorts and sweater.

'Grandad didn't feel too well, you remember? So the doctor sent him to hospital where they'll make him better. He'll soon be home, as good as new,' she told him simplistically, mentally touching wood. 'But Mummy will come for you very soon, and until she does you and I will have lots of fun. Now,' she lifted him down from the table, 'I'm going to make a pot of tea. Perhaps you could show me where the cups are kept? And would you like a drink of milk?'

'Juice,' he stated firmly. 'An' biskits. An' where's the man?'

He must have strong recall of the way Luke had taken him in his arms, holding him, comforting him, and Annie repressed a wry grimace. Was no one immune to the odious man's spurious charm? But his concern for the child hadn't been spurious, she reminded herself honestly, as she poured orange juice and rummaged through cupboards until she found the biscuit tin. It worried her, the way part of her wouldn't allow herself to dislike and distrust him as much as she knew she should. She didn't like the civil war that was going on inside her head.

And even before he spoke she knew he'd entered the room because the whole atmosphere altered subtly, enfolding her, wrapping her in a heated awareness. And that was something only Luke Derringer could do to her. A *frisson* of half-fearful excitement tingled its alarming way through her body and she stiffened, staring fixedly at the kettle she'd just slid on to the Aga hotplate.

'It seems he's "as well as can be expected",' Luke said drily. 'But I managed to get them to admit he's holding his own. And that's some consolation. Or don't you think so?' he added when she made no reply but continued to stare at the kettle as if she'd never seen such an interesting object before.

'Yes, I suppose so.' She forced herself to speak, then turned reluctantly to face him, to see his face lighten with the smile that had the power to melt bones as Jamie scampered towards him, holding out his chubby arms to be lifted, chortling as he was caught and tossed up against the big man's shoulder.

'I could do with that tea,' Luke told her affably as he sat at the table, bouncing the gurgling child on his knees, and Annie turned back to the chore in hand, foolish and unfathomable tears stinging at the back of her eyes. He was doing his utmost to make the best of a difficult situation, acting as though he found it perfectly normal to be isolated here with a woman who'd made it plain she despised him, wanted nothing to do with him.

The equable front was, of course, solely for the child's benefit. And when Jamie was safely tucked up in bed for the night Luke would turn his unwanted attentions to her! It was a terrifying thought. She couldn't hide behind the Professor because he, poor man, wasn't here, and Jamie would cease to be a barrier when he'd been put to bed. Something would have to be done about it. Despite despising Luke for his patently dishonourable intentions she knew, to her shame, that he would only have to touch her to have her craving for the magic she would find in his arms.

Her face paler than normal, she took two mugs of tea over to the table, putting his down at his elbow, cradling her own in hands which annoyingly and persistently shook. Keeping her voice light, her tone friendly because she didn't want Jamie to pick up bad vibes, she told him, 'You may as well leave as soon as you've had your tea.' She sipped at her own, ignoring the slow, knowing smile, the almost imperceptible shake of his head. 'We don't both need to be here to look after one small boy,' she tacked on firmly, 'and I'm sure there are plenty of business matters crying out for your attention.'

Now talk yourself round that, she thought, then listened, flattened, as he did just that.

'There's nothing that can't wait for a couple more days, and I wouldn't dream of leaving you to cope on your own. And in any case——' he ruffled Jamie's glossy dark curls '—two heads will be better than one. What I know about looking after children could be engraved on the head of a pin, and I dare say you don't know much more.'

It was almost a question and, carefully, she didn't answer it. She drained her mug instead and carried it over to the sink. She was about as knowledgeable on the needs of a three-year-old child as she was on the internal workings of a spacecraft! She had had a peculiar childhood, never staying in one place long enough to make friends, to be absorbed into another's family life and to come into contact with younger members of any family.

But she wasn't going to explain that, or anything else about herself to him, and it was apparent that he wasn't going to budge on his stated intention to stay put, so she would be wasting her breath if she tried to make him change his mind.

But she could, and would, distance herself. She said, 'I'll let Norman know what's going on,' and swept out of the room, taking her time about phoning because time spent away from Luke was time well spent.

Eventually, though, she settled herself on a leather chair behind a cluttered desk in what had to be the Professor's study. Like all the other ground-floor rooms she had just poked her nose into, it was high-ceilinged and spacious but in here, at least, an effort towards comfort had been made.

A fire was laid in the cavernous hearth and there were a couple of shabby but comfortable-looking armchairs. She wondered whether to put a match to the kindling and decided against it. Luke could light a fire and spend the long evening in front of it if he wished. She would take herself to bed as soon as Jamie was asleep. And she would lock her door.

With that thought on her mind she dialled, her fingers shaking, and she wondered disgustedly what had happened to her to make her feel so afraid, so vulnerable. Luke might torment her with words but he wouldn't force himself physically where he wasn't wanted. But perhaps, the intolerably honest thought popped into her mind, perhaps he already knew he was wanted!

She caught back a groan as Joan's voice cut out the dialling tone. She had expected to speak to Norman, had actually forgotten he was lying flat on his back in bed, and was guiltily amazed by how little she had thought of him since she'd left Seabourne in Luke's company.

'Oh, what a shame!' Joan's sympathy was patently superficial. 'I'll pass the message on, and of course you must stay as long as you're needed. There's no hurry for you to get back here. I've made Norman nice and comfortable. I got the man next door to carry the television through to his bedroom, and my armchair, so we'll both be able to watch together after we've had supper. I'm giving him his favourite home-made tomato soup and a nice piece of grilled sole...'

Which only goes to assure me that I am totally unnecessary to Norman's well-being, Annie thought as she murmured non-committal responses in what she hoped were the right places. Norman didn't want romance, and if he thought he was being offered the passion of a lifetime he would be appalled. What Norman needed was a wife who would look after his creature comforts, unravel life's knottier threads and be a compatible companion. Joan, she realised, was far better suited to that role than she.

And was he necessary to her well-being? Annie asked herself as she settled the handset back on its cradle. The answer was no.

She pushed herself up out of the chair and stared with empty eyes at the shabby, book-lined room.

She and Norman had decided to marry for various reasons, all of them sound. Companionship, a secure and settled home life based on a mutually caring relationship. Mutual respect. But since the business of Monk's Hall the respect had disappeared. It had been the cornerstone of her regard for him, and now that it had gone the whole edifice was crumbling. And since Luke had appeared on the scene she had been seeing sides of Norman's character she had never noticed before, sides she didn't like. Luke, with his personal and highly potent magnetism, had made her see herself in a new light, too, perhaps opening her eyes to things about Norman she didn't like.

She knew then, with quiet certainty, that she would never marry Norman.

'Come and get it!' The loud masculine call, closely echoed by a piping treble, penetrated the thickness of the study door and Annie lurched out of her introspective mood, a frown of annoyance darkening her eyes as she remembered her earlier decision to explore the upper regions after phoning her news home.

She had been determined to pick out a room for her own use, and stow her gear, before facing Luke again. But it would seem he had rustled up a meal and she would have to go back to the kitchen, if only for Jamie's sake. She and Luke had to make things seem as normal as possible.

In direct contrast to her own bleak thoughts the kitchen was bright and welcoming. Wondering at herself, she allowed her qualms, her mental reser-

vations regarding the devious Luke Derringer to slip
out of her mind quite effortlessly.

Informing herself that she was going to act as
though everything was hunkydory for the next half-
hour or so, simply because Jamie had suffered
enough traumas for one day without her adding a
hostile atmosphere to his suppertime, she wrinkled
her nose and said, 'Something smells good.'

Jamie announced gruffly, 'Luke's cookin' our
dinner.'

'Is that so?' Annie's smile was dry. She was already acquainted with several sides of his multi-
faceted personality, and had imagined various
others—none to his credit! But never would she had
added 'domesticated' to her list.

'His lordship,' Luke tilted his head in Jamie's
direction, 'placed the order. I hope you like fish
fingers, baked beans and noodles.' He turned from
the Aga, a slotted spoon in one hand, a frying pan
in the other, and his grin was devastating. It made
his face impossibly attractive. Annie flinched as her
breath caught in her throat, but she gave back his
smiling, appraising glance with a detachment she
was proud of.

He had, she noticed, opened the neck of his shirt,
and he looked hot, but not bothered. She was the
one who was bothered, she thought resignedly as
she scooped Jamie up in her arms and carried him
over to one of the dressers where she busied herself
by rummaging through the drawers for cutlery.

'When are you going to grow up, Annie, and lose
your need for a shield?' Luke enquired pleasantly,

and she stiffened immediately, setting the child down on a chair and hoisting it near to the table.

She wasn't going to dignify that taunt with an answer. The trouble was, she admitted tiredly to herself, he was right. Oh, not about the need to grow up, she was completely adult, thank you very much, but she had used Jamie as a shield, picking him up, showing him how to lay the table, acting as though Luke weren't in the room, talking to Jamie because she didn't want to admit that Luke was here, admit that he existed. He posed a threat, and that was something she would prefer to pretend to ignore.

But Luke wasn't so easily deterred. He had doled the unsophisticated ingredients of a meal on to three plates. Serving Jamie first, Annic felt his eyes on her, heard his low tones as an invasion of her mental privacy.

'What is it that makes you so desperate for safety? Does Willa Kennedy have anything to do with it?'

She accepted the plate he handed her with a stiff murmur of thanks, staring at it, feeling nauseous. Individually, the items of food were perfectly cooked; it was the combination she couldn't stomach. Or him. He would be enough to put her off the most delicious fare ever created.

'Am I right?' he persisted, taking the chair opposite hers.

'Of course not,' she answered coldly. 'I happen to be adult enough to appreciate security and the contentment that goes with it.' Not grown-up, she simmered, enraged at his poking his nose into her life as if he had rights!

'So you like to feel secure and content?' He lifted a fork, toying with noodles. 'That's a pretty boring ambition for someone of your age.'

So she was boring now, was she? Hot colour burned along her cheekbones, only to intensify when her stormy eyes lifted to meet the indisputable humour in his. About to burst with rage, she acknowledged that she had to cool down. She could hardly do as her instincts prompted. Jamie would be understandably distressed if she were to empty the contents of her plate right over Luke Derringer's head!

So she ate what she could of her meal in silence, only half an ear on the animated conversation being conducted between the man and the boy. Luke lost no opportunity to torment her and she couldn't think why. He'd admitted an interest in her, only sexual and fleeting, of course, but if he had seduction on his mind then surely he was going about it all the wrong way!

Almost guiltily, she stole a glance at him from beneath thick dark lashes. His was the face of a man who appreciated women. The cool blue eyes, the high-bridged nose, the sensual curve of his lower lip, reinforced her opinion. This was a man who would revel in sensuality, who would demand an answering response in his women. And his women, she reminded herself, would last no longer than his needs, his interest. He travelled far and he travelled alone; he made no commitments. Norman had told her that much, and nothing Luke had done or said in any way altered that opinion.

So what was it with him? She wasn't particularly beautiful and she most certainly didn't possess the glamour he would go for—glamour such as Willa possessed in abundance. So it must be the challenge of the chase and the inevitable conquest that drove him to torment her, she thought sickly. And when she'd succumbed, as he was so arrogantly sure that she would, he'd walk away. Nothing was surer than that.

There was a nausea inside her that had nothing to do with the meal Luke had made. The wall she had built around her emotions was beginning to crumble at the base—she knew it, and the knowledge made her feel physically ill. And it was all his doing. He had made her far too aware of the sensual side of her nature, the side she thought she'd battened down many years ago.

So she'd simply have to reinforce the hatches, she told herself forcefully, making Jamie's empty plate, his flushed cheeks and drooping eyes the excuse she needed.

Rising and taking the child's limply curling fingers in hers, she said brightly, 'Will you come and help me find a bedroom, Jamie?'

When he slid off his chair, his little hand tightening around hers, she added, 'Then it's bedtime for you—and me, too. Say goodnight to Luke.'

She didn't turn as she and Jamie left the room. She didn't need to register the sardonic 'Here we go again!' look that would be occupying those vivid blue eyes. She could see it all too clearly inside her head.

There was a slip of a room right next door to Jamie's, just big enough to house a single bed and a chest. Annie looked around and told Jamie, 'It couldn't be better. If you wake in the night, just give me a shout. I'll be right next door.' For all she knew, the little boy could well have nightmares about what had happened earlier in the day and she would be near enough to offer comfort quickly.

Returning him to his own room, she looked down at him uncertainly. She supposed he should be washed. She didn't think he was old enough to do it for himself, not properly, anyway, so she suggested, 'Why don't you show me where the bathroom is?'

But he ignored that, stating as firmly as a plaintive vocal wobble would allow, 'I want my mommy!'

'She'll soon be here, old son, I promise.' Luke had appeared in the open doorway and, annoyingly, all Annie could feel was relief. He scooped the small boy up in his arms, saying, 'I think I saw some bottled bubbles on the bathroom shelf. Did you bring them?'

He was already walking away down the corridor, the boy clinging to him, his hot little face buried in the man's neck. But he muttered, 'Yes, I brought bubbles.'

Luke went on, 'Then I guess they're there to be used. When I was your age, I seem to remember being bathed at the drop of a hat—when I got up, when I went to bed, and whenever I got dirty in between, which seemed to be an awful lot——'

'Did you have bubbles?' Jamie wrenched back his head to stare into Luke's face and Annie, trotting behind with the pyjamas she'd found under the little boy's pillow, found herself wondering what Luke's home life had been like, what his parents had been like.

It was a new consideration. Somehow she'd thought of him entering the world as a fully grown, adult, arrogant male! But he hadn't, of course. He had a background, like anyone else. And while he was running the bathwater, adding prodigious amounts of bubbling essence, she undressed Jamie and found herself asking questions, aware that she shouldn't be interested in anything about him, not if she intended to keep him firmly at a distance— which she most assuredly did.

'Are your parents still alive?' Somehow, she didn't doubt that they were. Only a vigorous couple could have produced this vibrant man, instilled in him that unquestioning self-assurance, that obvious sense of self-worth. 'Do you see much of them?'

"They're very much alive!' He had rolled his sleeves up and was testing the water, swishing the suds to mountainous heights. 'But I don't see as much of them as I'd like. When my father retired he and Ma joined friends of theirs in Vancouver. Dad and Joe spend most of their time fishing while Ma and Joe's wife try to outdo each other when they give dinner-parties. They're all having the time of their lives.'

His tone was indulgently affectionate, and she envied him his obviously caring background. But her eyes were fixed in unwilling fascination on the tanned, sinewy forearm which was gently stirring the water. Droplets of moisture clung to the slight furring of dark hairs, slicking them against the satiny skin that covered solid muscle and bone.

Annie gulped. Something was stirring to life inside her, uncoiling, then tightening. Quickly, she tore her eyes away and began folding Jamie's clothing as Luke lifted the child into the bath and reached for a bar of soap, gently rubbing the squirming body, grinning at the shrieks which ensued when Jamie found the bubbles coming up to his diminutive chin.

Watching the way Luke cared for the child—a delicate balance of firmness and indulgence—Annie's eyes sparkled with incipient tears. He was very gentle yet very masculine, and that was an alarmingly potent combination...

'And your parents? We all know and love the great Willa Kennedy, but what about your father? I know he died fairly recently, and I'm sorry about that. But did you get to spend much time with him?' He turned from his ministrations, his back still bent as his strong hands steadied Jamie's wild slides up and down the length of the bath. His eyes were holding hers, and there was more than a casual question in those deep, blue depths. He seemed to be reaching for her soul.

Annie didn't like the feeling of being dissected. If anyone else had asked that question she would have shrugged it aside with a casual half-truth. With this man, though, she was uneasily aware that she might just tell the whole truth, tell him that she'd never seen her father, that he'd never wanted anything to do with her, until right at the end when he'd willed everything he had to her.

Luke was dangerous, she admitted, almost drowning in those steady eyes. She had known that at the first moment of seeing him. She had to get a grip on herself. Her feelings were her own, weren't they? It would be folly to share them with him, to allow him to get closer to her.

If he had cared for her, and she had cared for him, she would have willingly have told him about her lonely childhood. But all he cared about was the chase, the conquest, and he would use any information she gave him about herself to serve his own devious ends! She didn't trust him; he was shallow.

So she said blandly, 'Spend much time with him? Not so as you'd notice,' and smiled. And her smile felt painful, as if it had been nailed to her face, and she was thankful when Jamie shipped half a gallon of water out of the bath and on to her feet, glad to have the excuse to break the steadily mounting tension, glad of the excuse to escape Luke's hypnotic presence. Her voice was oddly breathless as she made for the doorway.

'I'll fetch my things up from the hall and get into something dry.'

*   *   *

Later, when Luke had finished reading to Jamie from a story-book he'd found on the bedside table and Annie had changed into a long, woollen housecoat which zipped from her neck to her ankles, she poked her head round the bedroom door.

She had heard the soothing murmur of his voice trail off into silence, heard the snick of Jamie's bedside light and guessed the child was asleep. So now was the time to say her own goodnights. That way he wouldn't come looking for her, that way he would understand that she had no intention of spending a long, cosy evening with him!

'I'm turning in now,' she announced firmly. 'And I've mopped up the mess in the bathroom, so it's all yours now.'

'Is that so?' A half-smile tugged at his mouth. He advanced, just a little, very slowly. Annie felt colour rise to her face as her heart began to race frantically. He was altogether too potent, too male, too knowing. It frightened her.

She made to turn away, to close the door right in his face if that was what it took, but he reached out a hand and took her arm, stopping her in her tracks.

'I want to talk to you.' He sounded reasonable, not coaxing, not that, not from him. But reasonable, very relaxed.

She felt her skin burn beneath his fingers, the thick fabric no barrier at all. Her blood clamoured in hectic response to his magnetism. And she wanted to cry because she was losing something, she knew she was. And if she didn't move, didn't put an end to this—this whatever it was that drew her so strongly to him—there would be no going back for her, not ever.

She wasn't going to lose her self-control, her self-respect, her peace of mind, for the tawdry, all-too-fleeting excitement of physical pleasure. Years ago she had made that vow to herself and she wasn't going to break it now. When she gave herself to a man it would be because she loved him, and he loved her. She was capable of loving—despite Willa's off-putting example. And, in a blinding flash of insight, she realised that Luke, in some strange way, had taught her that much about herself. Had taught her that one day she would meet the man she could truly love. And she knew that that was the reason she had really decided to break with Norman. She had never loved him and never would.

'Please let me go. I can think of nothing you might want to say to me that I might want to hear.' She tried, she really tried, to sound uninterested, but her voice emerged throatily, and he grinned slowly, as if he knew that the words her brain strung together had nothing whatsoever to do with what her body was saying.

'I might surprise you.' There was an infuriating edge of laughter to his voice and, far from releasing her, he pulled her closer. She could feel the heat of his body now, and, desperately, she pulled back, her movement violent, knocking her head on the doorpost so that she winced, biting her tongue against crying out with the sharp pain because she wouldn't permit him to see such weakness.

'Surprise me? Not you,' she hissed, the sharp, transitory pain in her head fuelling her anger. 'I can read you like a book. It begins with the chase and ends with the conquest and there's nothing else. No substance. Nothing!'

'And that is exactly why we have to talk.' His mouth had tightened fractionally but his tone was quiet, level, as if he remembered the sleeping child so close at hand. 'We have a lot of talking to do, you and I, and we can't do it here.' He reached behind her and closed her bedroom door. 'Fighting me won't achieve a thing—unless it's another self-inflicted blow on the head. So you come willingly' —his words were dangerously soft—'or I'll carry you and let you face the consequences of un-avoidable bodily contact! The choice is yours.'

# CHAPTER SIX

SOME choice! Annie fumed silently. She could scream and yell and wake Jamie, but that wouldn't be fair, or kind, to the child. Or she could silently resist and find herself scooped up in those strong arms, held closely against that hard male body.

She had no choice, none at all, and she trudged sullenly at Luke's side, determined at least to handle whatever came next with dignity. A quiet, self-contained dignity was the only defence she had left.

'In here.' He didn't touch her; he simply stood aside as he opened the door to the Professor's study, motioning her to enter. He was being cagey, handling her with polite reserve, but she didn't know how long that state of affairs was likely to last. She didn't trust him an inch.

He had put a match to the kindling and the fire was burning well now, the flames making a curiously comforting pattern of mellow light and shade on the book-lined walls, aided only by a single, low-wattage table-lamp.

It was warm in here, the wind that rattled the casement windows serving to emphasise the cosiness of this particular cocoon. But she wasn't going to be lulled into a false sense of security.

Taking the initiative, she sat in the armchair facing the fire, tucking the long skirts of her robe demurely around her legs.

'Well?' she questioned with a hint of asperity. 'Say what you want to say. I'm tired and I told Jamie I'd be next door if he woke and needed me.' She hoped he couldn't detect the way her heart was thumping.

'He'll be out for hours,' Luke said with irritating confidence. It was on the tip of Annie's tongue to tell him he was talking through the top of his head, having already admitted he knew little of the ways of children. But she contented herself with one withering glance. She wasn't going to pick a fight. Coolly and unemotionally was the way she was going to play it.

Her scornful glare elicited only the merest flicker of humour before he passed in front of her to toss another log on the fire. Then he straightened, dusting his hands off.

'I want to talk to you and we're going to be very adult and civilised about it. Both are qualities you pride yourself on having, aren't they, Annie? That being so,' he casually draped himself into the chair adjacent to hers, 'you should be perfectly at ease.'

At ease! she thought scornfully. She would be more at ease alone with a cobra! Already the tension—sexual, she had to admit—was getting to her, and she had been alone with him for less than five minutes! It made her feel disorientated, out of her depth, and she wished he would say what he wanted to say and get it over. Instead he just sat there, watching her, giving her the uncomfortable impression that he was privy to her secret thoughts, was able to get inside her body, to directly detect the rate of every last pulsebeat. And, later, she was to recall someone once saying, 'Never make a wish—you might just get it granted!'

'So...' He looked totally relaxed, his elbows on the arms of the chair, his eyes lazing over steepled fingers. 'So when do you intend breaking your engagement to Norman?'

His effrontery in asking that question, as if he had every right to know, took her breath away, set her heart pattering against her ribcage. Conveniently forgetting that here, in this very room, only an hour or so ago, she had realised that she could never marry Norman, she replied nastily, 'I don't. Not that it's any business of yours, of course!'

'I'd say it was very much my business,' he gave back, disconcerting her.

And was it her imagination, or had those deceptively lazy eyes become dangerously narrowed? Annie couldn't be sure, but just to be on the safe side she told him more pacifyingly, 'I'm afraid your logic escapes me. Now, if that was all you wanted to say, I'll go to bed.' She made to rise, her instincts—always highly tuned where he was concerned—warning her that she was on dangerous ground.

'That was just for openers,' he informed her briskly, his eyes impaling her so that without being aware of how it had happened she was sitting down again.

But she was very aware of the way her mouth had suddenly gone dry and of the way he was now looking at her, as if daring her to move a muscle.

Her pulses skittered erratically but from somewhere she dredged up enough control to regard him with a mixture of weary patience as he began to tell her, 'If you marry Norman you'll be making the greatest mistake of your life. Can you truthfully say you love him, that you could share the intimacies of marriage with him, sleep in his bed, and not wonder what it would have been like with me?'

The studied look of weary patience fled. Of all the conceited, self-opinionated, vile——! She had had her temper under control until now, and she recognised how very close she was to losing it completely. But a supreme effort had her primming her mouth as she countered him acidly.

'If I make mistakes then that's my problem, not yours. But I can tell you I'd never make the mistake of giving you a second's thought—in any capacity whatsoever.'

'Wouldn't you?' His voice was velvet-smooth, and she watched with terrified fascination as he left his chair and moved towards her, silently, like a cat. Her heart almost stopped beating and she knew that if he intended to prove his point she would be powerless to lift a finger to stop him.

'I wonder.' The richness of his voice was a caress, enough in itself to overpower her senses, and a *frisson* of bitter-sweet sensation coursed through her as he reached out and lifted her to her feet.

'Does Norman's touch make your flesh grow weak?' he asked silkily. 'Can his mouth blind you to reason? Can his hands make you remember there's a passionate woman behind that prim exterior?'

He wasn't touching her, just holding her an arm's length away, but his voice was touching, his eyes were touching, exploring every inch as if he could see clear through the thick barrier of her robe.

Her body felt on fire. She had never felt such primitive desire for a man before. With his eyes, his voice, he was capable of bringing forth a feeling of abandoned wantonness that hadn't surfaced for years.

And she had never felt quite like this before, certainly not with Norman, dear, dull Norman. Not even with Hernando, whom she had wanted with all the hedonistic desire of a seventeen-year-old.

But beneath her fear of him, of what he could do to her, was emerging an unquenchable excitement. And that was terrifying because it meant that she had no control over her own body, not where this one man was concerned. But she did have the use of her brain, she reminded herself muzzily. She had to attack him verbally, it was the only defence she had. She drew in her breath roughly, forcing out her words.

'You make me ill!' Fighting now, she wrenched her arms from his grasp, her eyes furious, rejection of him, of the way he made her feel, boiling in her blood. 'You're everything I despise in a man. You're a conceited, arrogant creature! Not content with trying to seduce your own cousin's fiancée behind his back,' she choked, tears of rage making her eyes glitter, 'you've bought the loveliest house in the area for the sole purpose of adding it to your chain of pocket-lining hotels. I hope you're proud of yourself!'

'Good,' he said softly, astonishing her. She had expected him to retaliate, to show anger at being thwarted. But, infuriatingly, he looked pleased with himself, satisfied even. She was the one out of control, hurting, the one who couldn't think straight through the amalgam of outrage, confusion and downright hatred that boiled in her brain.

Tears were streaming uncontrollably now, almost blinding her. But she had too much pride to wipe them away. Stumbling, she made for the door, unwilling to spend a moment longer in the same room as her tormentor, but he was there before her, barring her way, and compassion gentled his voice as he said huskily, 'Poor Annie, poor baby.'

And that was all it took to have her sobbing, gulping back the shaming tears, totally vulnerable because no one, ever, had spoken to her in that tone. It was as if her pain was his, as if he really cared. For one of the few times in her life she didn't feel emotionally alone.

She didn't know how she came to be in his arms, but she was. And it felt good, as if she had come home after a long, cold journey. He was rocking her gently and she could feel the warmth of him, feel his steady heartbeat against the rapid pattering of her own, feel the softness of his shirt beneath her splayed and suddenly heavy fingers, smell the clean male scent of him.

His breath was warm against the softness of her cheek as he said, 'I had to get you angry enough to give yourself away. I had to try to get at the truth, sweetheart.'

Little by little he was easing her back into the comforting ambience of the fire-glow, and she hadn't the strength or the will left to resist him, to stamp her own authority on this dreamlike interlude. She didn't know whether she had any authority left to stamp around, she thought hazily. Her flesh was quivering, melting, where it met his lean, rangy body. Their clothing seemed no barrier at all where sensation was concerned.

'What truth?' Her mind had difficulty in forming the question which that enigmatic statement of his seemed to demand. All that really concerned her now was the sheer physical bliss of being held, held so very tenderly, by the man she had called her enemy.

There was no enmity now, simply a warmth, a softness, a certainty. All her life she had wanted to feel she belonged—to a person, to a place. She had learned to live on the surface of life, coping with those unfulfilled longings, realising that no one had the right to expect to have everything they wanted. And now, strangely, she felt she had come home, that home was in this man's arms.

His hands were gentle on her body as he sank down on a chair and pulled her with him. Cradled within the warm curve of his body, held by the caring strength of his arms, she made no protest when he stroked his fingers through the bright softness of her hair, fitting her head into the crook of his shoulder, his lips soft and undemanding against the quivering curve of her own. And she knew she hadn't the wit, the energy, or the desire to protest against anything he might do.

'You think you hate me because I threaten your dull, safe relationship with Norman,' he told her throatily. 'But most of all, I suspect, because I beat you down over Monk's Hall.'

His mouth moved against hers, a gentle, teasing ghost of a kiss, a kiss fragmented into a thousand tiny, tantalising movements of skin against skin, almost taking, almost tasting, an erotic glimpse of what could come. She couldn't focus her mind on his words, only on his mouth as it touched hers, withdrew and touched again...and again.

'You feel no passion for Norman because you don't love him and because for some reason known only to yourself you distrust sexual passion.'

Gently, taking her by surprise, the tip of his tongue trailed sweet moistness between her lips, dipping just slightly into the soft corner of her mouth, and her hands clutched his body convulsively as sheet lightning sensation rocked her.

His lips withdrew, moving slowly to the tip of her nose, her eyelids—each fluttering in turn beneath that infinitely seductive male mouth. Achingly, she longed for more, much more than the tantalising kisses that promised so much, withheld so much...

Her body was compliant, pulsing with frantic need, aching, wanting...

Only moments before she had been hating him and he had reduced her to unthinking, illogical rage, reduced her to tears, and now reduced her to this. And, strangely, it didn't matter now. The chemistry, the magic between them, was far more powerful than she could ever have believed possible. And he was telling her things she shouldn't want to hear, shouldn't want to know.

'So you sublimated all the sexual passion Norman couldn't answer into a pile of bricks and mortar— Monk's Hall. And, as you see it, I took it from you. And so you think you hate me for it. But you don't hate me at all, do you, Annie?'

She was almost prone in his arms now and his mouth dropped to the pulse that fluttered rapidly at the base of her throat, and she couldn't have argued with him to save her life.

'You want me, Annie, as I want you. But you're afraid to admit it.' His fingers had found the top of the fastener that secured the swamping robe she wore and, inch by slow inch, he slid the zipper down until the curves of her high round breasts were revealed for his lingering appraisal. 'I'm going to teach you not to be afraid of your sexuality, to welcome it,' he told her huskily, and she tried to shake her head, to deny that she was in any way afraid at this moment, that she would welcome his lovemaking with every fibre of her being. But the effort of speech was beyond her and she instinctively opened her mouth for his kiss as his head descended, her fingers reaching up to thread convulsively through the crisp darkness of his hair.

This time the kiss went deep, utterly beguiling her, turning her trembling body into one endless ache of yearning. In a small, almost forgotten corner of her mind she knew she was betraying herself, betraying her long-held principles. Sickened by her mother's example, she had always promised herself that she would only make love with a man if there were a long-term commitment on both sides. Casual sex was not for her. But, oddly, even that didn't seem to matter. Nothing mattered but the precious magic of what was happening between them.

She felt as if she had entered another plane, a place where nothing had substance but this sweet ravishment of the senses, the promise of sublime fulfilment.

Slowly, tantalisingly, he drew down the zipper, exposing the satiny length of her body to his shadowed eyes, and then those eyes raised to meet hers and they were smouldering with desire as he said thickly, 'Let me love you, Annie,' and her lips parted on a sigh because she knew she couldn't say no.

One word would have ended it now, she knew that, but she was incapable of saying that word and her lashes fluttered submissively on to her cheeks as the dark head bent to hers.

The subtlety of his mouth's exploration was sheer luxury, and she was trembling with a need she hadn't known existed in such intensity as his hands travelled ravishingly, learning the shape of her, the texture of her. She knew that soon she would be his, and she savoured that knowledge because she knew that something within her had changed, and soon now, very soon——

'Annie! Annie!' She was to wonder, later, at the incredible shrillness of a child's voice at night-time. 'Annie—I wanna wec-wee!'

Luke's breathing had been ragged, his body very still, in that moment before he had put her aside, very gently, and raised himself to his feet.

'I'll go,' he'd told her, his eyes on fire as he'd traced a light finger over the bruised outline of her lips. 'This shouldn't take long.'

But long enough for her to come to her senses.

Feeling as if a bucket of ice-cold water had been emptied over her, she struggled back into her robe, her fingers fumbling with the zip, almost falling over herself as she crammed her feet into her slippers.

The interruption of one highly successful seduction scene had been farcical, to say the least. She wondered if Luke had ever had such a thing happen to him before. She would lay odds he hadn't!

Like the women who would have attracted him, such scenes in the past would have been smooth as fine old brandy, highly sophisticated, glamorous.

He might have known that with *boring* Annie Ross things would be very different! She didn't know why he'd bothered, she thought savagely. And she didn't know whether to laugh or to cry, so she settled for being ashamed of herself instead.

And shame kept her awake for most of the night, one ear pricked for any further sound from Jamie's room. At some time, not long after she'd crept into bed and burrowed deep within the blankets, Luke had tapped lightly on her door and she had growled, 'Go away! I hate you, Luke Derringer!' and he must have heard because he'd gone away without attempting to open the locked door.

But most of all she hated herself. How could she have been so despicably weak? For years she hadn't been troubled by physical lust—which was what she felt for Luke, she assured herself.

When a smooth, dark Spaniard with eyes like liquid coal had intoxicated her with his golden voice, his expert hands, she had been besotted enough to ignore the lessons learned from her mother's behaviour—that pathetic and constant pursuit of so-called love. But Willa had noted her daughter's blossoming, had soon discovered the reason for it, and had taken Hernando from her with shaming ease.

Willa had had to prove herself irresistible, prove that no man would look at another woman while she was around. That the other woman had been her daughter, and that her young heart might have been broken, hadn't counted.

For weeks Annie had believed her heart was broken, but that had been excusable. She had been just seventeen.

But there was no excuse now, none at all. For seven years she had known better than to trust mere physical attraction, knowing that there had to be more, something much deeper, if a relationship were to last. And yet all it had taken had been a husky voice, a pair of deep blue eyes, a lean and powerful body, and there she'd been—on the point of begging him to make love to her!

His taking of Monk's Hall was as nothing to the way he had taken her pride, the respect of self she had so carefully built over the last seven years.

When at last she fell asleep she was out for the count, and only woke when a battering at her door had her opening bleary eyes to Jamie's yell of 'Wake up, Annie!'

And then Luke's deep tones, informing her that it was gone ten, set her insides lurching uncomfortably. Pulling on the robe which now had such shameful memories, she wondered how she was ever going to face Luke again after what had happened.

Gingerly, she unlocked her door and shot back the bolt. She had put up barriers where none had been needed. Luke would never have forced himself on her, no matter how aroused he had been. She had to respect him for that. For at that moment she respected him more than she respected herself, she decided uncomfortably. One word from her would have had him backing off. Just one word, and she hadn't been able to say it. Hadn't wanted to say it!

Satisfying herself that the males in the establishment had taken themselves off, she hurried to the bathroom, stood under the shower and wondered what to do. The events of last night wouldn't go away, no matter how hard she wished they would, so she would just have to take him aside and firmly inform him that it would never, could never, happen again.

So she dressed in the neat grey suit she had brought with her to bolster her research assistant image when working with the Professor, and stared at her subdued reflection: hair neatly slicked back, face wearing only a modicum of make-up, expression suitably aloof. All very well, but would Luke accept her ploy? Would he believe that whatever madness had overtaken her last night would not be repeated?

Probably not, a nasty little inner voice told her, reminding her that during each successive confrontation between them she had given just a little bit more—and he had been quick to take what was offered! He had, she recognised sickly, adroitly led her by the nose—and she, poor sucker, had suspected nothing! But now was the time to call a definite halt. It was up to her, she knew it was, and she would do it or die in the attempt!

Apart from a slightly raised dark brow, Luke gave no hint of surprise at her choice of formal gear. He put a steaming mug of fresh coffee down on the table and asked, 'Would you like toast? Eggs?'

'We had our breakfast ages ago!' Jamie scampered up to her and flung his arms round her knees. 'Luke said not to wake you 'cos you'd had a heavy night. What's a heavy night, Annie?'

'Late to bed,' she lied, hating herself for blushing because she knew that had Jamie not felt an urgent call of nature her night would have been very heavy indeed!

Wordlessly, she shook her head at Luke's offer of breakfast, meeting his eyes just briefly before flicking her own away. She had seen something in those deep blue depths that had turned her bones to water.

Getting a hold on herself, she picked up her mug and cradled it gratefully between cold hands, wondering how she was going to get through the rest of the day if she only had to meet his eyes to go weak at the knees. So her relief was enormous when Jamie piped, 'My mommy's coming today!'

'She phoned from Birmingham about half an hour ago,' put in Luke. 'She was lucky and got a flight almost immediately. She should be here by lunchtime.'

'Great,' Annie muttered thankfully against the rim of her mug. Another twenty-four hours here, cooped up with that devil, had been something that had made her shake just to think about.

She caught his eyes on her, humorously narrowed, and swallowed the unaccountable lump in her throat with the remainder of her coffee. Today he had chosen to dress in black—a lightweight, body-hugging black sweater, narrow-fitting black denims. The sombre garb didn't make him look menacing or predatory—just devilishly attractive, and she wished, for one shattering moment, that he weren't the man he was.

Why couldn't he have been more like Norman? Norman wasn't the love 'em and leave 'em type, whereas Luke didn't know the meaning of the words commitment and fidelity! She would be plain crazy to fall into his arms for the brief affair he had in mind—no matter how much she desired him physically. He was obviously a womaniser of the worst possible kind. No man who would attempt to seduce his own cousin's fiancée could have an honourable bone in his body!

Briskly, she emptied her mind of such maunderings. He was a loner, uncommitted to anything but his work, and any relationship she entered into would have to be long-term.

'Professor Rhys is out of intensive care now, and making good progress,' Luke told her, following her to the sink where she was making a minor production of rinsing her mug.

'You phoned the hospital?' Her hands stilled suddenly, her voice emerging huskily. He was too close; his nearness made her shake inside.

'No, they sent smoke signals,' he responded drily, making her feel a fool. And worse than a fool. Useless. While she had been sleeping as though drugged, he had been up, giving Jamie his breakfast, contacting the hospital. He was a caring, re-

sponsible man, she had to give him that, and the
admission shook her. And it puzzled her, too. She
couldn't easily equate the caring side of his character with that of the devious seeker of immediate
satisfaction he had proved himself to be. And, in
any case, it would have been easier to continue to
think of him as irresponsible, uncaring, intent
merely on self-gratification.

She stood rigidly at the sink, the mug clasped
between her hands, willing him to go away, to give
her space to breathe, but he took the mug from her
to hang it on the dresser, smiling faintly as if he
knew how much he troubled her. And now was as
good a time as any to come out with her carefully
prepared speech. Jamie had disappeared so there
was nothing to stop her, but although she opened
her mouth no words came out.

Luke said, 'Jamie and I will be going for a walk.
Won't you join us?'

The voice was coaxing, very warm, and through
the window she could see the wide expanse of blue
sky, a rugged snatch of landscape glittering gold
and silver and green beneath the sun. And she was
almost tempted until, his eyes raking her as if he
could see right through the prim grey suit to the
soft body beneath, he continued, 'Though I would
suggest you get out of that defensive garment first.
It's not much good for hill walking, or anything
else.'

And that did it. It reminded her that she
shouldn't willingly go anywhere with him!

'You go ahead,' she replied tartly. 'I'll get a room ready for Jamie's mother and make lunch. She's bound to be feeling washed out when she arrives,' she qualified stiffly, 'with all that travel and worry.'

She hadn't meant to make it sound as if he were callous, going out to enjoy himself while she stayed behind and worked. But it came out sounding that way and she could have sworn a flicker of distaste—and disappointment?—moved across his face before he turned away.

'Suit yourself. I'd planned on being back in plenty of time. We could have done everything necessary together.'

Together. The word imprinted itself on Annie's brain, made her throat feel tight. It held promise and pain in equal measure. Being the people they were, togetherness was out of the question, she knew that perfectly well. So why did she suddenly want to cry?

Pans were bubbling on the stove, the study fire was blazing well and coffee was percolating by the time Paula Fellows arrived. And Annie was able to tell her the latest news.

'Your father's well on the road to recovery. Luke phoned earlier, and I enquired again about half an hour ago. You can go and see him whenever you like.'

'Thank God for that!' Paula's face was ashen with fatigue and her grey eyes brimmed as she told Annie huskily, 'I can't thank you enough for stepping into the breach. I can't think what would have happened to Jamie otherwise.'

'Mrs Morgan would have taken him with her,' Annie assured her quickly and, sensing that total collapse was imminent, suggested firmly, 'Coffee, I think, by the fire. Then lunch. After you're rested I'll drive you to the hospital.'

In the event it was Luke who drove Paula to see her father while Annie played a strange hybrid of cricket and football with Jamie on the grass in front of the house. His reunion with his mother had been ecstatic. 'Where's Daddy?' he had demanded at last.

Paula, still inclined to be tearful, had told him, 'He'll be here tomorrow afternoon. He couldn't get a seat on the same flight and he's going to have to hire a car.' She had passed a shaky hand over her forehead, glancing up at Luke. 'I honestly don't know whether I'm coming or going.'

At least Jamie will be tired out by bedtime, Annie thought, as she watched the small boy dive into a thicket of rhododendrons after the ball she'd just hit. Then she lifted her head as she heard the approach of the Ferrari.

At the sight of the tall figure unwinding itself from the driver's seat Annie's heart performed a lurching somersault. Making herself tear her eyes away from him, she walked over to the shrubs, peered into the dusty depths and called, 'Your mommy's home,' disgusted to hear how husky her voice was.

Damn the man! she agonised as she watched the child emerge, his face streaked with dirt, his fat little legs seeming to fly over the ground as he headed for the car. Luke made her feel like a young girl in love, and she wasn't a girl and she wasn't in love and she was going to have to do something drastic about it.

But what? a weary inner voice enquired as she slowly made her way back to the house. What indeed?

# CHAPTER SEVEN

IT WAS dusk. The mountains were far behind them, and the countryside showing up in the Ferrari's headlamps seemed tame by comparison. But the atmosphere inside the car wasn't tame; it was tense, almost electric.

Paula had been adamant about her ability to manage on her own.

'There's no need for you to stay a moment longer. My family's imposed on you both too much already. And Jim will be here tomorrow.'

She had been a different woman after seeing for herself the rapid progress her father was making.

'And I'm going to put my foot down about Dad living here alone,' she'd stated, battle lights glinting in her eyes. 'He knows Jim and I would love to have him live with us—there's ample room for him and all his books, and Jamie adores him.'

'So all's well that ends well,' Luke commented, uncannily taking up Annie's train of thought, before adding, with that maddening confidence of his, 'And that's the way it's going to turn out for us.'

For a moment her heart seemed to stop and a sharp visceral pain knifed through her. He obviously believed she had given him the green light last night, that her later repudiation of their earlier intimacies had stemmed from a coy, virginal need to draw breath. So now, this minute, was the ideal time to put him right.

Drawing in a ragged breath, she stared straight ahead, her eyes fixed on the headlights as they cut a dazzling swath through the twilight.

'Nothing will end for us because nothing ever began,' she stated through stiff lips. Her mouth felt numb, as if she were gradually turning to a block of stone. Weird, she thought wildly, that the verbal act of denying the strange immediacy of the disastrous attraction between them should make her feel as if she were slowly dying inside.

But she was a sensible woman and she sure as hell wasn't going to have an affair with him, and she folded her hands in her lap and stoically waited for his blistering comments.

None came. And his voice was smooth as silk when he eventually replied, 'Lie to me if you must, but don't lie to yourself, there's a good girl. You can't be an emotional coward all your life.'

Apprehensively, she darted a sideways look but his features—or what she could see of them in the dusky interior—were as equable as his voice as he continued with damning veracity.

'Something began for us at the precise moment we met. Had it not, then I would simply have decided that Monk's Hall was suitable for my purposes, made a duty visit to The Laurels as I was in the area, paid my respects to Norman and his future wife, then returned to town. One of my deputies would have sat in on the auction and I probably wouldn't have set foot in Seabourne until the Monk's Hall project was completed. I don't keep dogs to do the barking myself. But I saw you and something started, something I couldn't fight, didn't want to fight.'

He glanced at her briefly and, even through the gloom, his electric-blue eyes reached her, touched her soul, made her shake.

'I'm being as honest with you as I know how to be, so why can't you be honest with me, Annie?'

'I am being,' she lied. Suddenly the issue of what he intended to do with Monk's Hall didn't matter any more. It hurt, but it was no longer the catastrophe she had believed it to be. Catastrophic emotions only emerged when one cared deeply, and perhaps he had been right and she had been sublimating her sexual drive into a pile of bricks and mortar. The central issue now was his shameless and openly acknowledged pursuit of seduction— her seduction! And that could turn out to be a catastrophe of monumental proportions if she ever allowed it to happen. An affair, for him, would be nothing more than a pleasant interlude in a busy life, nothing more meaningful than that. But for her, making love with him would mean loving him, and it wouldn't be meaningless at all. And if she allowed him to make love to her, with no love on either side, then she would be degrading herself, and she couldn't live with that.

'Last night is something I'll always be ashamed of,' she informed him stiffly. 'It can't and won't happen again.'

A sharp hiss of indrawn breath was his only response as with one swerving movement he hauled the car off the road, braking viciously on to a lay-by, gravel spurting beneath squealing tyres. And for the first time ever she sensed a terrible anger in him, his former patience with her clearly a thing of the past.

His reaction to her repudiation of him frightened her. Until now he'd always been in control, his management of her—and that was what it assuredly had been—light and easy, if sometimes a little acid.

But there was something dark here now, something furious and demanding, and the face he turned to her was grim. But his anger, although it was real, was controlled and he asked her tightly, levelly, 'Do I have to make you angry again before you'll tell me what this is all about? I think we could both do without the trauma, don't you?'

'In case you'd forgotten, I happen to be engaged to Norman and I don't want a sneaky affair with you!' she countered hotly. 'Why can't you get that into your head?'

'But you are going to break with Norman, aren't you?' he stated unequivocally, and she stared ahead into the darkness, her body rigid, and told him, 'No,' flatly, because she wasn't going to give him the satisfaction of knowing he was right.

'And when that's behind you,' he went on grimly, as if she hadn't spoken, 'there'll be time for us. Because, whatever happens, you're going to be mine.'

'Oh, am I?' she choked, unnamable emotion clogging her throat. 'For how long? Until you tire of me? That's just great, isn't it?' she snorted, disgust with him, with the way he could churn her emotions, sparking her anger. 'You'd be willing to break up what Norman and I have, just because you've decided you want me to share your bed for a while? You've got to be the most selfish, unprincipled bastard I've ever met!'

'Maybe,' he acknowledged tautly, his fingers drumming an angry tattoo on the steering-wheel. 'But I want you, and Norman doesn't—not in the sense I mean. And, like it or not, you want me, so why the Victorian scruples? In any case, all Norman is to you is a father figure. Think about it.'

He started the engine and drew the Ferrari back on the road, seemingly unaware of her now, of her shocked reaction to his declared intent to have an affair with her. And that, more than anything else, ignited an unreasoning anger in her.

How dared he blithely assume she was like all the other women who had been willing to share his bed for brief periods of time! How dared he! He might accuse her of having Victorian morals, and maybe she had, but she just wasn't hard enough, sophisticated enough, to take casual sex in her stride, to shrug and walk away when the footloose loner re-emerged, when he tired of her and moved on to seek fresh challenges, new conquests.

It was fully dark when they reached The Laurels. Luke entered ahead of her, anger riding him still.

'Break with him. Tonight,' he commanded tersely, stalking to his room, leaving those few words hanging in the air like a threat.

A hot denial gathered in her throat and she longed to scramble after his lordly, retreating figure and scream that no way would she do a single thing he commanded her to, because she was her own woman, always would be, and she certainly wasn't his!

But a brawl like that would only alert the others to his outrageous behaviour and make hers sound as bad. Better to swallow her ire, her need to retaliate, and simply ignore him!

Swallowing her rage, she walked slowly to Norman's room. She could hear the unmistakable sounds of a Western clear through the door.

Tonight she would break their engagement, but not because Luke had told her to. She had to do it for her own sake, and for Norman's. Almost regretfully, she recognised the change in herself that made marriage to Norman no longer possible.

Luke had taught her that she was capable of passion. Luke was wrong for her, of course; she had no intention of gratifying his whim for a short-term affair. But one day the right man for her might come along and then, she knew, she would be capable of a deep and enduring love. So she would break their engagement and she knew, without a doubt, that her only emotion in the aftermath would be one of relief. Knew, too, that Norman would not be hurt. Maybe his pride would suffer a little to begin with, but even that might remain untouched because his emotions had never been involved, either.

She pushed open the door, the retort of rifles, the drumming of hoofbeats, which issued from the set drowning out the sound of her entry.

Norman and Joan were absorbed, her armchair pulled up at his bedside, a box of chocolates on the counterpane between them. They looked the archetypal middle-aged couple, contented and comfortable with each other, the knowledge of the other like the knowledge of self. And in that moment, before her presence was noted, Annie prayed that Norman would eventually see where his best hope of companionship and undemanding happiness lay. Joan would make him a far better wife than she could ever have done herself.

She moved, caught their attention, saw Norman register surprise—nothing more—and recognised something hostile in Joan's eyes before she got up and lowered the sound.

'We didn't expect you.' Norman sounded almost annoyed and Annie, smiling politely, perched on the end of his bed.

'I should have phoned, I'm sorry. Anyway, how's the back?'

'Improving slowly.' He smiled at her then.

Joan, though, rushing around collecting their used coffee-cups, put in, 'Have you and Luke eaten? If you'd bothered to let us know when to expect you, I could have had something ready.'

'Not since lunch,' Annie told her. She wasn't particularly hungry herself, but Luke might be, though why that should bother her she didn't stop to analyse. 'I'll fix something for him, you carry on watching your film.'

'Certainly not.' Joan sounded huffy and Annie shrugged. If Joan wanted to play the martyr then there was little she could do about it.

'I'll have a quick wash,' Annie excused herself. 'Then I'd like a word with you, Norman.' Pushing herself off the bed, she made for the door, but Joan's voice stopped her.

'Your mother phoned, by the way.'

'Willa?' Annie went very still, her hand frozen on the doorknob. Was her mother straining at the bit to take a look at the man little Annie had caught herself? If so, she thought drily, she was too late.

In any case, Norman was one of the few men around who would be impervious to Willa's wiles. And was that, she thought with a flash of bitter insight, why she had agreed to marry him in the first place?

The idea shook her, made her look at herself in a new and unfavourable light, even as Joan said, turning Annie's preconceptions upside down, 'She left a message. She wants you to go to her. She's in Capri—at her villa, she said.'

'Did she say why?' Annie's brow furrowed. Her mother had never really wanted her around. From her teens she had been pushed well into the background of the famous star's life because having a grown-up daughter made her less youthful in the eyes of her admirers. There had to be something drastically wrong to make Willa need her.

'No.' Joan was plumping Norman's pillows, smoothing the counterpane. 'No, she didn't. But she sounded distraught. I think you should go.'

Only because it suits you to have me out of the way, Annie decided cynically. But after this evening Joan would no longer see her as a rival.

'I think I should go, too.' She gave Norman an enquiring look. After all, he was still her employer and could claim her time until she'd worked out her notice.

'Yes, you must,' he agreed readily. 'Take all the time you need.' He didn't seem perturbed by the thought of her absence—in her capacity either as his research assistant or as his fiancée. 'I shall be confined to the house for what could conceivably turn out to be weeks, and the new project's postponed, of course. How is the Professor, anyway?'

The enquiry was belated, but it deserved as full an answer as she could give and five minutes later she left him, going to her room to collect her washing things, a change of clothing.

Of Luke there had been no sign. Maybe he was still too furious with her to feel like socialising with the others, she thought. But there was no sign of anger in him when she practically bounced off him as he came out of the bathroom door. There was something dark and hot in the eyes that met hers and it terrified her more than his anger could ever have done.

All he wore was a towel draped low round his hips, and her mouth went dry. He was magnificently male, lithe, no spare flesh on his muscular frame, his skin velvety, tanned, darkened with rough hair.

She stepped quickly aside, her face scarlet, her pulses hammering a wild tattoo, and he reached for her, his voice raw as he pulled her tightly against the shocking warmth of his nearly naked body.

'Understand me, Annie—I want you, need you. And there's no going back, no forgetting, not now. It's far too late for that.'

She stood still in the warm circle of his arms, her body melting. His magic scuttled all her resolution, as if those firm thoughts and intentions had never existed. Then his hands slid up to cradle her head, his fingers splayed in the softness of her vivid hair, gentle fingers, gentle hands, gentle enough to make her shudder with clamouring needs of her own. And softly, he kissed her, his tongue feathering her lips until she opened them to him, quite voluntarily, desire, deep enough to come near agony, unfurling violently within her.

He could call forth this need at will, she recognised wildly, and she was helpless against his potent persuasion. Helpless, doomed by the wantonness he could command from her.

Convulsively, her hands gripped the naked breadth of his shoulders, feeling solid bone beneath the pliant muscle and heated flesh, and a moan escaped her as he withdrew his mouth from hers and said huskily, 'Enough. Enough for now, my love. Later there will be all the time in the world. And then I will take you and love you with kindness, with passion, with utter devotion. And you will learn what it is like to touch the stars.'

He said those words as if she had no say in the matter, and perhaps she didn't, she thought, beginning to panic, caught in the oldest trap in creation.

She muttered something incoherent, the words sticking thickly in her throat, and hurled herself through the bathroom door. Fumbling for the bolt, she shot it home, then leaned back against the cool, painted wood, her eyes closed, her heart pounding frantically.

Sickened, she knew that he could have taken her there and then, such was the blinding magic of his touch. His bedroom door had been a mere yard away and she would have gone with him, given herself to him without reserve or shame. The shame would have come later.

But he had held back, spoken about a future that would never be theirs. She wanted to cry. She wanted him. She wished she'd never met him.

'You look tired.' Norman's smile was faintly sympathetic.

Annie said raggedly, 'I suppose I am, a little.' She was more than tired, she felt as if she'd been put through a mangle. Her emotions had taken a monumental pounding during the last few days.

Coming from the bathroom she had caught a glimpse of Joan and Luke in the kitchen, preparing supper, and she knew she didn't have much time. So she said quickly, as gently as she knew how,

'Norman, I'm sorry, but I can't marry you. It wouldn't work out for either of us.' Her eyes were wary as she saw distaste darken his face.

'It's Luke, isn't it?' he stated grimly.

'No, of course not!' Shock roughened her voice. 'What makes you say that?'

'I say that because I'm not a fool,' he snapped. 'It was more than cousinly interest that kept him around here before the auction. He's a busy man with usually more than a dozen irons in the fire at any given time. He wouldn't have been hanging around if there hadn't been something in it for him and I saw the way he looked at you—as if he could eat you with his eyes.'

'Yet you were perfectly willing for him to go with me to Wales,' Annie snapped right back, appalled that Norman should have so accurately read his cousin's intent and yet done nothing about it.

'I trusted you,' he countered darkly, then went on peevishly, 'I needed the transcripts of those interviews, and the photographs. And I thought you were too level-headed to be taken in by that womanising relative of mine. But you spent two days alone with him and come back to break our engagement—so what do you expect me to think?' He looked surly, like a thwarted schoolboy.

Her face fiery, her eyes volcanic, Annie ground out, 'Luke has nothing to do with it,' and knew it wasn't the complete truth. Luke had demonstrated that she was capable of deep emotional feeling, a sexual need that Norman could never begin to satisfy.

'I don't believe you,' Norman stated huffily. 'And don't imagine,' he shot as she made to leave the room, 'that you'll tame the brute. You won't be the first woman, or the last, to believe she's got what it takes to get him to make marriage vows and mean them. He's too greedy. He likes quality and quantity when it comes to women. So if you think he'll offer marriage and permanency, then think again. I've known him for thirty-odd years and you've known him for a handful of days. And, I'll tell you now, he'll never marry you!'

'My heart bleeds!' Annie snapped sarcastically, but, sweeping out of the room, she knew her words held a smattering of literal truth. She was breaking up inside, but didn't know why.

Norman hadn't needed to spell out the truth for her. She knew just how shallow Luke's interest in her was, and was pretty certain that once she was out of his dangerous orbit she would forget him, forget the wild magic of his touch. So why did she feel as if her heart were bleeding?

But she would be leaving first thing in the morning, she told herself grimly. She would take the first available flight out to Capri and as far as Luke was concerned she would have vanished off the face of the world. His world, anyway!

# CHAPTER EIGHT

'SHE'S sleeping. It's the first proper rest she's had in two weeks. I don't want to disturb her.'

'Of course not.' Annie didn't take offence at Nora's brusque welcome. A grim, plain dragon of a woman, Nora Gooch had been with Willa for over twenty years, all the devotion she was capable of going to the temperamental star. No one else had ever got a look in.

It was Nora who guarded Willa against importunate fans, snarling directors, the demanding Press. She who soothed and cajoled when Willa threw a tantrum, who grumbled unceasingly over Willa's wilder excesses, who applauded each and every performance the star gave—on screen or off—boosting an ego that was already dangerously inflated.

'I'll show you your room.' Nora strode ahead, her flat shoes flapping against the cool marble floor. 'She hoped you'd come, and I'm thankful you did.'

And that was one big concession, Annie thought, as she lifted her suitcase and followed Nora up the curved staircase.

The usual poky room she had been allotted on past occasions when she and her mother and the usual entourage had stayed at the villa was not for her this time, Annie noted with a faint lift of one dark, arching brow. Nora was showing her into one of the sumptuous guest-rooms, all clear lemon silk curtains and bed-coverings, the carpet a deep-pile pure white.

'You're going to have to fend for yourself,' Nora informed her dourly, her brown-clad bulk planted in the centre of the room. Against the delicate, elegant background the older woman's uncompromising plainness appeared incongruous. 'She dismissed all the servants, gave her secretary an unlimited leave of absence and cancelled Griff's visit.'

Annie's heart sank. Willa, in one of what she called her 'states', always demanded an audience. If Willa were depressed, enraged, or even merely bored, then as many other people as possible had to be in on the act, to witness the performance, had to soothe and placate, amuse and sympathise, had to turn themselves inside out in the effort to make her feel happy and pampered again. And Griff, her agent, was more adept than most when it came to coaxing Willa back into a sunny mood. He was more than half in love with his illustrious client and, for that reason alone, was always the first to be called in a crisis, the first to come running.

But if his visit had been cancelled there had to be something very wrong indeed.

'What's going on?' Annie moved over to the windows and looked down on the wrinkled blue silk of the Mediterranean.

'The end of a love-affair.' The older woman sat down heavily on a fragile-looking gilded chair, staring glumly at her broad, capable hands. 'In the past she's always been the one to end it. She gets bored, or finds someone else and moves on. You know the pattern as well as I. This time it was different. *He* ended it.' Her mouth turned down in a look of distaste. 'I did warn her. He was less than half her age. A pretty Dutch boy who only wanted one thing—a part in her next film. She hasn't been able to take it. It broke her up and, as if that wasn't bad enough, your letter arrived announcing your engagement. She'd just lost a man and you'd found one. She's no spring chicken, Annie,' Nora imparted drearily, 'and I think she was plain simmering jealous of you.'

A toy boy! Annie felt her knees buckle as distaste and pity in equal measure enervated her. She walked slowly across the room and sank down on the edge of the silk-covered bed, feeling the mattress dip beneath her slender weight.

'So she sent for me?'

Annie's mouth went dry as Nora put her inner misgivings into words. 'Naturally, she's burning to find out what manner of man you've managed to capture!' She got heavily to her feet. 'One word of warning—keep him away from her, at least until some new and fascinating man walks over her horizon.' Her voice deepened, and her words were heavy, as if they were being dragged from her against her will. 'She hasn't treated you well—I've not been blind to her faults over the years. She'll make mischief if she can. At the moment she's a bitterly unhappy woman and she'll try to take your happiness from you. She won't see it that way, of course.' She paused, her hand on the porcelain doorknob. 'If she took your man from you she'd tell herself it wasn't her fault, pout her lips the way she does and say she can't help being totally feminine, completely irresistible! Now...' she sighed tiredly '...I'll go to her. When she wakes I'll tell her you're here.'

As soon as she was alone Annie moved briskly about the room, unpacking her case and putting her things away. The content of Nora's warning hadn't surprised her, only the fact of its delivery did that. In the past Nora had treated her as if she were invisible, and her devotion to Willa had been such that she wouldn't have warned her own mother if the star had taken it into her head to do that lady a fatal mischief!

However, the warning was invalid, Annie thought drily as she dumped folded underwear into a drawer. She no longer had a fiancé!

A quick shower in the adjoining palatial bathroom freshened her a little. The flight to Capri had been relatively short but she felt jaded. And that was owing to her fraught emotional state, she admitted, sighing as she pulled on a pair of light cotton jeans and a cool, matching, apricot-coloured top.

Flicking a comb through her hair, she caught her full lower lip between her teeth in an effort to stop it quivering. Every time her thoughts turned to Luke, wondering where he was, what he was doing, how he had taken the very final slap-in-the-eye of her sly departure, she felt like crying.

She didn't know why he should be so difficult to get out of her head. She had left Seabourne without a word to him, leaving no forwarding address because putting distance between them was the only sensible thing to do in the circumstances. She was missing him more than she could have thought possible.

But at least Willa's problems and the dismissal of the servants meant that her time and her mind would be fully occupied, leaving little room for Luke to intrude.

But he did intrude, damn him! Mentally, he dogged her footsteps as she wandered through the large, silent villa. Through airy rooms and quiet corridors thoughts of him nudged relentlessly at her mind. And she couldn't stand it!

Roses—she would pick some for her room. Even in autumn they bloomed in their thousands in the magnificent, cypress-enclosed gardens that swept via green-lawned terraces to the sea.

But no sooner had the thought occurred than Nora appeared in an arched doorway.

'She wants to see you. I've just made a pot of tea—take it with you and try to persuade her to have some. She's been living on uppers and downers for the past week.'

'Of course.' Automatically, Annie followed Nora to the kitchen, her eyes skimming the laden tray with disbelief. Willa would never allow herself to sample those buttery scones, that wickedly rich chocolate cake. 'Don't you think she'd be more tempted by a thin cucumber sandwich or a very small green salad?' And then, seeing a look of distress pass over Nora's normally deadpan face, she added quickly, 'But I'll gorge myself on your delicious baking, I promise! It is yours, isn't it?'

'Since she tipped out the servants, cook and all, I thought I'd make the type of stuff I fancy for a change.' Nora held out the tray and balanced it on Annie's hands, a twinkle of humour in her eyes. 'I'll fix something less fattening for her ladyship, though in my opinion she could do with gaining a stone.'

Annie had too many memories of her mother's indifference to her to feel anything less than apprehensive as she carried the tray to the room Willa always used when staying at the villa. And compounding her anxieties was the very real fear that the actress had suffered a breakdown.

Everything pointed to it. There was her uncharacteristic insistence on being alone—it was unheard-of for her to live without a troop of servants. Even when she came to the villa to 'get away from it all', as she would wistfully announce, she had always demanded a full complement of admiring hangers-on.

And, equally obviously, Nora couldn't cope. Why else should she have admitted to being thankful to see Annie—have confided in her to the extent that she had done?

Gingerly, Annie nudged the bedroom door open with her knee and stood in the doorway, hardly able to believe her eyes. The curtains were almost completely drawn across the windows, but even in the dim light she could detect the squalor of the frowsty room.

Willa had always been so fastidious, both in her person and her surroundings, and the surly-eyed woman who regarded her from the depths of the rumpled bed didn't look like the glamorous, sophisticated Willa Kennedy at all. She looked old, she looked lost and she looked broken.

Swallowing around a painful lump in her throat, Annie advanced with the tray, and cleared a space on the table-top.

Willa said thickly, 'So you managed to tear yourself away from your fiancé at last.'

'I came as soon as I could.' Now wasn't the time to explain about the broken engagement. The most pressing consideration right now was to ascertain the seriousness of Willa's condition. She might need medical help. 'I've brought some tea,' she went on calmly. 'I'm gasping for a cup myself. But I think we could do with a little more light.'

She went to the windows briskly, pulling back both sets of curtains, wincing inwardly as she saw the full extent of the damage. Cosmetic pots and bottles had been hurled in a tantrum and lay where they had fallen, spilling their contents on to the priceless Persian rugs. The heavy peacock-blue satin bed-hangings had been clawed from their fitments and lay in shimmering pools over the floor, the bed. But worst of all was Willa.

Annie had never seen her mother look anything less than perfect and she doubted if anyone else, save Nora, had either. Now her blonde candyfloss hair was lank, her skin blotchy, her brown eyes puffed with weeping. She had lost weight, too, and the loss had aged her.

Petulantly, Willa waved aside the cup of tea Annie offered and whispered huskily, 'I feel as if I'm finished. You might as well know it—everyone else does by now.'

'Is that so?' Annie sipped from her own cup, her oval face impassive. She had heard those particular phrases too often before to be unduly alarmed. She knew she was now expected to state that the star had never looked lovelier, more fascinating, that her last role had revealed greater depth and range than any that had gone before and that her rich vein of talent could only improve.

But when she had left Willa to make her own life she had vowed that never again would she be one of those called upon to spend long wearying hours flattering the star's ego. She wasn't about to go back on that vow now. She would do all she could to help but she wouldn't employ the worthless tactics of flattery.

'You don't care, do you? Willa said spikily when Annie made no reply but calmly helped herself to a slice of Nora's chocolate cake. 'You just don't understand, but then you never did. I don't know how to tell you, but there's more——'

'There always is, isn't there?' Annie interrupted firmly. Another good hour's worth, at least! And it was time she directed a few constructive home-truths towards her mother. Flattery, even if it were sincerely meant, would not help Willa out of the depression which was, Annie hazarded, more genuine than any of those she'd claimed to suffer over the years.

Leaning back in her chair, she said levelly, 'You certainly will be finished if you go on the way you are now. But if that's what you want, then go ahead—shut yourself in here, starve and neglect yourself. That way it won't be long before you've completely lost your looks and the only parts you'll be offered—that's if you're in any state to take them—will be tottery old grandmothers!'

'Bitch!' The empty water glass from the bedside table missed its mark, smashing against the wall several feet away from Annie's head.

Annie swallowed a smile of relief. Willa was back on form! It was the first positive response her mother had made since she had entered this room. And although Annie hated hurting her she knew that Willa had benefited more from those few plain words than she would have done from any amount of pleading or flattery. And, much as she loathed having to do it, she pressed on.

'I don't think the defection of a self-seeking pretty boy is worth the destruction of a legend, do you? But if you think it is,' she continued remorselessly, hating what she was doing yet seeing no other way to shock Willa out of this self-destructive mood, 'then go on exactly as you are. It shouldn't take too much longer to make the damage irreversible. But if you've got half the sense you were born with you'll begin picking up the pieces, starting now. You're no longer young enough to indulge in this kind of tantrum and emerge physically unscathed.'

Annie disregarded the blackly hostile expression of the woman in the bed and began methodically to tidy the room, folding the fallen bed-hangings, picking up the scattered debris of pots and jars, flinging one window open to let in the sweet fresh air. And all the time her heart was aching for the silent woman crouching in the big bed. For all she knew she might have made matters worse, but she had had to try.

Willa had been a poor parent by any standards, but she was Annie's own flesh and blood and she couldn't walk out on her now. Besides, she thought with a trace of defiance that had her lifting her chin, she loved her, metaphorical warts and all!

But her heart was in her mouth as she advised, 'If you put your mind to it you can come out of this room looking a million dollars, and in a few days' time you can throw one of those glitzy parties you're so good at and let everyone know that the great Willa Kennedy doesn't go to pieces because a silly boy got ideas way above his station.'

Trying to disguise the tremor in her hands, she emptied the cup of cooling tea, poured a fresh one and put it into her mother's hands.

'Drink this for a start. I'll go and see what's keeping Nora. She was bringing something to tempt your appetite.'

Outside in the corridor she leaned weakly against the closed door. Willa hadn't uttered a word since she'd called her a bitch and hurled the water glass.

She'd just lain there, her puffy eyes sullen, listening to the kind of things that no one, but no one, had ever dared to say to her before.

But at least she'd accepted the cup of tea. That hadn't been hurled at the wall! Annie hoped that was a good omen.

'How was she?'

Annie hadn't heard Nora's approach and she started visibly, a slender hand flying to her throat.

'I—— Heavens, you made me jump!'

'That bad, was it?' Nora remarked drily. 'Was she pleased to see you?'

'Not that you'd notice,' Annie responded ruefully, pushing herself away from the door. 'I told her a few home-truths, tidied up a little, and——'

'Bully for you!' Nora's eyes widened in grudging respect. 'She's made that lovely room into a pigsty and yelled blue murder if I tried to put it right. Think she'll eat this?'

Annie considered the dish Nora held. Succulent fresh prawns lay on a bed of crisp lettuce, and were garnished with tiny cubes of tomato and cucumber, lightly coated with a delicate dressing and accompanied by very thin slices of brown bread and butter. It looked delicious enough to tempt anyone, but . . .

'Goodness knows. But if she does eat it we'll know the battle's won. Good luck!'

Muttering darkly, Nora tapped on the bedroom door and pushed it open. Annie, wandering downstairs to get a much-needed breath of fresh air, hoped that all would go well. But beneath her very real concern for her mother her emotions were taking on a strong life of their own. They had nothing at all to do with Willa and everything to do with Luke.

For the first time in her life she had actually pitied Willa, and out of that pity had sprung understanding. Not of Willa, but of herself. Ever since she could remember—apart from that brief and traumatic affair with Hernando—she had been determined not to emulate her mother's lifestyle, her giddy affairs, her numerous marriages, her perpetual pursuit of the illusion of love.

But what if love wasn't an illusion? What if love, true love, could be real and earthy, solid and sound?

Willa had never been able to settle for one man, but had been too busy searching for a perfection that didn't exist, fated by some emotional flaw that refused to allow her to accept that life, even love, could not forever be perfect, a high romance. No man or woman was ever perfect, and real love, devoid of immature illusions, gladly adored the loved one's good points while learning to accept the not so good.

Had she, she wondered restlessly, been wrong to run from Luke? The astonishingly strong sexual chemistry between them could so easily have turned to love, on her part, at least.

Restlessly, she moved through the hours of the lazy afternoon, Luke walking through her mind. She wouldn't have believed it possible to miss someone so much. Her whole body ached for him. She felt sick and tearful.

She was on the point of phoning The Laurels in the vain hope that he might still be there when she admonished herself to grow up. All he wanted from her was a short-lived affair, a glorious but fleeting gratification of the senses. And so, no matter how her body responded to his, she couldn't go along with that. She couldn't be stupid enough to lay herself open to that kind of heartbreak.

She had done the only sensible thing. She had put distance between herself and the overwhelming temptation he offered. So why—away from his beguiling eyes, his magic touch—was she totally unable to put him out of her mind?

# CHAPTER NINE

'SHE'S doing wonderfully well, isn't she?' There was an almost maternal pride in Nora's voice as she carried the lunch tray in from the patio. 'And you can take most of the credit for that. I can usually handle her but I was out of my depth this time.'

'Nonsense,' Annie denied listlessly. 'Sooner or later she would have realised what a fool she was making of herself. Now, if you're sure you can manage, I'll drive into town.' The food she had already prepared for this evening's small party was stowed away in one of the giant refrigerators, and she needed to get right away from the villa for a while. Oh, how she needed that!

'Of course I can manage.' Nora plunged the lunch dishes into a sink of hot water. 'She's going to have to rest now and then I'm to give her a face pack and massage, and do her hair. I don't know, though...' Her busy hands stilled in the hot water. 'Is tonight's party a good idea? It's early days.'

'It's what she wants. She wants to prove to the few close friends she has around here that she's as good, if not better, than usual.' Annie gave Nora a reassuring smile and headed for the door. 'Don't worry so.'

Personally, the idea of one of her mother's parties—although a small one—appalled her. But

Willa had made a supreme effort to pull herself together and it seemed sensible to go along with her wishes, within reason.

Annie herself had no wish to attend the party tonight but she had to, if only to keep an eye on Willa, to see she didn't overtax herself or get upset by the type of vitriolic remarks her so-called friends were apt to come out with. Because although the star had made remarkable progress her nerves were still tightly strung.

And it would be a thankless task, Annie thought wearily as she slid behind the wheel of her mother's Porsche. Willa would resent the idea that anyone was keeping an eye on her, especially as it happened to be her daughter! Annie hadn't missed the ice in those big dark eyes, even though Willa had been superficially pleasant all day. No doubt she was still remembering the harsh truths Annie had come out with. The tactics had worked, but they obviously still rankled!

But to the party she must go; therefore a dress she must have. She had brought only a rudimentary wardrobe with her, and an afternoon's shopping might take her mind off Luke and the content of the dreams she'd had about him, which had been erotic enough to make her blush whenever she thought about them!

But nothing worked. Wandering through the little town left her mind freer than she wished. All day yesterday, and this morning, she had been at full stretch—organising the immediate return of the servants, arranging for Willa's secretary to report for duty after the weekend, making nourishing little meals to tempt her mother's capricious appetite, contacting Griff in the States, at Willa's request, to beg him to get himself over here post-haste, helping Nora to organise the food, drink and floral decorations for the party, issuing telephoned invitations...

Even busy, as she had undoubtedly been, she hadn't been able to stop thinking of Luke. The wretched man was becoming an obsession!

Sick of herself, she dived into the first boutique she came across and walked out less than ten minutes later, her purchases made with impatience and no pleasure.

She would drive back to the villa and go for a swim. A long, strenuous swim. It was a beautiful afternoon and the exercise might tire her sufficiently to dull her mind, to make her muscles ache so that the ache in her heart would blend in with all the other twinges and become unrecognisable for what it was.

After dumping her packages in her room she tapped lightly on her mother's door and obeyed the summons to 'Come!'

'Do you have a swimsuit I could borrow?' she asked, ultra-polite. 'I didn't think to pack my own.'

'But of course, dear. Nora will show you where they are.' The tone was sugary sweet but the brown eyes were frosty and Annie looked away from the graceful, kimono-clad figure reclining on the broad windowseat and glanced at Nora, who was busy with a box of heated rollers.

'Third drawer down in the white chest,' Nora instructed, then turned to Willa. 'It's time we got your hair washed if I'm to do anything with it.'

Running over the smoothly cut emerald-green terraces, a towel draped around her shoulders, Annie felt deep desperation claw at her, making her stomach churn, her throat burn tightly with unshed tears. She knew she was literally running away—from Willa's concealed resentment, from herself, from memories of Luke. The only trouble was, there was nowhere to run.

The sea beckoned, a glittering, crinkled blue silk, edged with lacy white foam, and Annie shrugged the towel away and felt stupidly self-conscious as the Mediterranean sun lapped lovingly over her almost naked body.

Willa's selection of swimwear had comprised a multitude of bikinis, not a one-piece in sight, and nothing to choose between them in the skimpiness stakes. She was slightly larger than Willa, practically everywhere, and she was sure she looked positively indecent in the tiny wisps of jade-green fabric.

But there was no one to see her, she reassured herself as her long legs carried her over the clean, honey-coloured sand. The beach was private, access between the high cliffs only gained through the villa's extensive gardens.

The water, when she plunged into it, felt wonderful, cool and silky against her heated skin, and she swam until her protesting muscles could no longer be ignored with safety and reluctantly waded out to face the rest of her life, a future without Luke, without love. Because love him she did. The knowledge came with shocking clarity.

She stood like a sleepwalker, disorientated. She loved Luke. She had found within herself a potential for deep, passionate, enduring love. And this was worse, far worse, than merely wanting him, because, for him, love didn't come into it.

Stunned, she recalled the vital immediacy of their attraction, how he'd only had to touch her to make her forget his manifold faults and respond as she'd never responded to a man before. She simply hadn't realised she was falling in love.

If, just once, he'd said he loved her, had spoken of marriage, of commitment, she would have accepted him gladly—she knew that now. She would have trusted her future to him because, days ago, her body had known what her mind had refused to accept. She had actively fought what she now knew was her growing love for him, but she had lost the battle.

And precisely what she was going to do about it, she didn't know.

And then she saw him and her heart stopped in its tracks. He was wearing narrow black denims belted low on lean hips, and a black sleeveless T-shirt which moulded his torso to aching perfection. His dark hair was ruffled by the offshore breeze, otherwise he might have been carved from rock, the incredible deep blue of his eyes steady, watching her.

Her stomach lurched over as her heart began to beat again, picking up speed, her pulses racing as she faced the unbelievable.

Had she conjured him out of her imagination? Was that still, silent figure there by some freak of yearning? A figment of a fevered imagination?

And then her heart turned over inside her, very slowly, with sweet, sweet painfulness, because he moved, he was real, and he was here. Standing motionless, too bemused by the sheer, blinding quality of her joy even to breathe, she watched him pace deliberately towards her.

His past didn't matter, nothing mattered but the glory of seeing him again, and she knew what people meant when they said that love was blind.

Sea-water was gently lapping her calves, gathering in glittering droplets on her skin, sticking her hair to her skull. And Luke walked through the water until he was standing over her and she smiled in simple ecstasy, her arms instinctively reaching for him and nothing had ever felt this right before.

'I ought to give you a beating. I never want to have to live through the past two days again,' he growled huskily, just before his arms gathered her nearly naked softness into the hard, impatient strength of his body.

The kiss seemed to last forever and yet it was nothing like long enough. It was as if soul spoke to soul through the fusing of lips, the erotic interplay of tongues, the desperate clinging of hands. And when he at last raised his head she stared at him breathlessly, her lips swollen and bruised, her eyes dark with love.

Sunlight glistened on bronzed skin covering hard muscles, was reflected from the depths of his eyes, making them glitter like precious gems. And his clean male breath feathered her skin as he muttered, 'When will I be able to get it through your skull? There's no point in running, Annie. I'll always follow you. Always.'

Emotionally overwrought, she felt her throat clog with tears and she said shakily, 'I can't run, Luke, not any more.'

She heard the sharp drag of his breath, saw the kiss-softened line of his lips part as he groaned, 'Oh, Annie, my love!' and then his hands were on either side of her head, his fingers splayed in her wet hair as his tongue explored the parted sweetness of her lips with a seductive promise that turned her blood to fire.

His body pressed urgently against her own, transmitting wildly clamouring messages. She received them open-heartedly, with joy. She loved him, she always would. Nothing mattered now but that. She could no longer fight the force of their mutual and shattering attraction.

His hands were moving over her heated flesh now, moulding her, exciting her almost beyond endurance as the floodtide of desire relentlessly pressured her senses, insistently, urgently demanding a release from the burning, aching need that possessed her, a need only he could satisfy.

'I couldn't believe you'd gone,' he muttered hoarsely, moving his lips from hers, his mouth trailing erotically along her jawline, from the hollow behind her ear to the point of her chin, feathering down the length of her throat, leaving a trail of burning sensation that had her clinging weakly to the strength of his rock-solid body.

Convulsively, her hands clutched at his chest, her fingers uncurling against the warmth of his T-shirt, the heavy beat of his heart transmitting its rhythm to her own as she began a fevered exploration of the hard, well-defined musculature of his body, his wide shoulders, the warm, tanned skin of his throat.

She was melting all over, disintegrating with her love for him.

He demanded thickly, 'Why did you run?'

'Because I was afraid. Because you're not my type,' she whispered, a catch in her voice as her mouth moved against his sun-warmed throat, and his hands tightened around her hips, pulling her close into his body, making her shockingly aware of how very much he wanted her.

'And what is your type?' he questioned thickly, his lips finding hers again, touching and tasting.

'It's not—not——' She could hardly speak, her voice was so thick with the force of the desire he was arousing. 'Not the whizzkid, entrepreneurial inhabitant of Glitz City type!' she managed, stumbling over the unmanageable words.

Clearly exasperated, he roughly drew her even closer, and answered, 'Do you always prejudge people? I assure you, I'm not a kid, and I never whizz, and if Glitz City exists I've never been there!'

'But I don't really know you,' she murmured, drowning in sensation. Not knowing him didn't really matter at all, not now. She had changed out of recognition, was prepared, as never before, to base her whole existence on love, to trust her emotions.

'Then we'll have fun learning about each other, won't we?' he suggested, scooping her up in his arms as the incoming tide crept around their melded hips. Carrying her, held close to his body, he lovingly laid her down on the warm sand, drinking in every exposed inch of her body with heated eyes.

Annie stretched luxuriously, unashamedly, her movements sensual, languid, watching him watching her as, with a few economical movements he removed his own clothing and she was filled with a strange wild ecstasy as she drank in the pagan magnificence of his superb male body.

Then he was beside her, his fingers tantalisingly slow as he removed the tiny scraps of fabric that partially covered her aching breasts. Then, slowly, he lowered his head, taking one hardened peak between his lips, his hands moulding her hips to the hard maleness of his, making her mindless with longing.

She whispered his name as his body covered her and he said rawly, 'Annie, I love you,' and the wonder of those words, the touch of the hair-roughened bronze satin of his skin, set her on fire.

Arching her body to his, she responded wildly, lost in the hot, sweet urgency of a desire she could no longer control or deny, a desire she now welcomed without reservation.

His breathing was deep, ragged, and her hands reached up, her fingers twining through his dark hair before languorously moving down over his shoulders, over the tight skin of his back, his ribcage, getting to know the shape of him, the feel of him. And, hungrily, his lips took hers, took her breasts, moving wildly, relentlessly, as if he wanted to devour the whole of her, one hand sliding along the heated silk of her thighs to effortlessly remove the tiny triangle of fabric that was the only barrier remaining between them.

'You're no longer afraid of love?' It was not exactly a question, more a statement, because he had to know now, after the ecstatic way she had followed him to the delirious heights of loving, that, for her, fear of unfettered emotion, of her own sexuality, was a thing of the past. Hadn't she, over the past overwhelmingly beautiful hour, shown him as much?

Wordlessly affirming what he already knew, she nuzzled her rumpled head into the crook of his shoulder as they walked slowly towards the villa. One strong arm held her possessively against his side, their bodies, where they touched, seeming to fuse.

Annie trailed the towel from one languid hand, unashamed now of the near nudity of her body.

She wondered how she could bear to be apart from Luke, even for the one night he had grudgingly conceded she must spend with Willa.

They had arranged that she would drive him to the village where he would find a room at one of the hotels, and then she would—with difficulty, she knew—return to the villa to do her duty at the wretched party her mother had decided to give. And tomorrow she would join him and they'd make plans. What those plans would entail he hadn't said and she didn't know. How far into the future he was looking was something she didn't dare to think about. But he had said he loved her and that was all she needed to know.

They were nearing the house, their footsteps growing slower as if both of them would delay the separation, however brief it was to be, and Annie asked, 'That yours?' meaning the single suitcase on the gravel sweep in front of the villa. She wondered if Griff had arrived, a full day earlier than he'd said he would.

'Uh huh,' Luke confirmed. 'I always travel light, but this time I threw enough gear together to last me for what might have turned out to be a protracted tour of Europe in search of a shapely, red-headed, stubborn female.' His hand tightened on the naked flesh of her slender waist. 'I dropped it where I stood when a large, dour woman told me you'd gone down to the beach.'

'That would have been Nora.' Annie smiled up into his eyes. 'She's Willa's minder. And tell me, how did you know where to find me?' It had seemed like a miracle when he had appeared on the beach and, as if she couldn't yet get to grips with the reality, she needed to have it explained.

'Easy. Joan told me.' His voice roughened as if he were in pain. 'When I realised you'd gone, without so much as saying goodbye, I nearly went out of my mind. It was as much as Norman could do to speak to me at all, let alone tell me where I could find you. But Joan took pity and came to my room while I was packing. She told me you'd broken your engagement and gone to your mother's. I guess that lady—Nora, did you say?— thought I was out of my head when I just dropped everything and ran for the beach. I hadn't hoped that things would turn out to be so easy!'

As if on cue, Nora appeared between the marble pillars flanking the main door.

'Willa wants to know if your fiancé would like to make use of the villa while he's here?' she said to Annie, her eyes openly assessing Luke's undeniably charismatic person.

Annie opened her mouth to deny the natural mistake, but Luke stepped forward, introducing himself, extending his hand, and Nora, to Annie's amusement, actually blushed when her own hand was swallowed by his.

'I'd be delighted to stay,' he said, smiling wickedly over his shoulder at Annie, leaving her in no doubt that he found Nora's mistake amusing and that he relished the opportunity for the two of them to spend more time together. He probably wondered why she hadn't made the offer herself, and she couldn't have explained why she hadn't, not in words that would have made much sense.

As Luke bent to pick up his abandoned suitcase a slight movement overhead caught Annie's eyes. Looking up, she saw the corner of a bedroom curtain drop back into place by the scarlet-tipped hand of a secret observer. Willa.

It was ridiculous to be feeling so apprehensive, Annie nagged at herself as she took a hurried shower. Willa had obviously been spying on them as they'd walked up from the beach, the time they had taken giving her ample opportunity to send Nora down with that message. But what of it? she mentally chided herself. It was only a natural interest in the man she mistakenly believed to be her daughter's fiancé.

But how interested was Willa? And what direction would that interest take?

Pushing the grumbling thoughts aside, Annie towelled herself dry. Luke had said he loved her and Luke wasn't another Hernando—besides, she was older now, more sure of herself. She could handle Willa!

Reassuring herself, she recalled how, when Nora had offered to take Luke to his room, she had mentioned that Willa wanted to see her. Annie had been expecting the third degree, but Willa had only mentioned Luke once, and that, as it were, in passing, saying in a barely interested tone, 'It's as well I happened to be sitting in my window when your fiancé arrived. Nora tells me he was going to take a room in the village. He'd have gone away with a poor opinion of my hospitality.'

She had gone on to ask Annie whether she should wear the blue or the grey, both simple, under-statedly elegant dresses, and Annie had said, 'The blue. The colour suits you so well.' And Willa had agreed, smiling, no frost in her eyes now, leaving Annie to wonder if her mother was really herself again, because she always made sure she shone brilliantly at any social gathering, and she wouldn't do that in either of the dresses she had picked out of her lavish wardrobe.

And for a moment Annie had hugged her, wanting to give her some reassurance because, just for a while, Willa had looked like a lost kitten. Amazingly, her mother hadn't pushed her away as she always had done in the past when Annie had tried to show affection, and that gave her even more reason to hope that things would be different this time. If she had changed during the past seven years, then so had Willa.

She hadn't bothered to correct the mistaken assumption that Luke was the fiancé Annie had mentioned in her last letter. The difference in the names had obviously not struck Willa yet, and the whole tangled story would take too long to tell, especially as her mother was anxious to get herself ready for when her guests arrived.

Fortunately, the dress Annie had picked out, almost at random from the rails in the boutique, suited her. Had she known that Luke would be arriving out of the blue she would have gone to endless trouble and probably still not bettered this one—the first dress in her size she had come across.

The turquoise chiffon flattered her vivid hair and creamy skin, and the scoop-necked bodice, held by a couple of narrow straps, fitted sleekly at the waist and hips and made the most of her slender yet curvy figure.

The simple style of the dress needed no ornamentation, and that was just as well, since she had left the few pieces she did possess back at The Laurels. And it was just as well that Willa had decided to dress simply tonight. If the star had elected to pull out all the stops, then she, Annie, would have been well and truly eclipsed!

Tonight was to be a simple affair all round, she reassured herself. Just a few of Willa's friends, all of them British expatriates who had made permanent homes in Capri. It would be nothing like Willa's wilder parties, the sort which had made Annie squirm in the old days. Nothing at all to feel apprehensive about.

'Darling! You look fabulous! Utterly divine, as always! We'd heard such *worrying* rumours about you——' The high-pitched voice shrilled from the open salon doors and reverberated around the spacious hallway.

Annie, reaching the bottom step of the curving staircase, recognised Jacinth's voice and smiled wryly to herself. The permanent Brits on the island formed a colony of sorts, and the rumours of Willa's collapse after being thrown over by her toy boy would have been bouncing back and forth among the section who formed Willa's circle, growing more outrageous with each repetition.

Willa, astute as she was, had invited the linchpins along tonight to prove she was as vital as ever, totally unconcerned by the departure of whatever-his-name-had-been! Annie had to admire her.

She would look gracious and sophisticated in the blue cocktail dress—a touch subdued, perhaps—but even so, the very antithesis of the slightly deranged, insecure middle-aged woman of a couple of days ago.

Willa had disappeared somewhere but all the guests had arrived, Annie noted as she walked into the salon, her heart flipping and flopping like a landed fish as she spied Luke at the opposite end of the long room. He looked breathtakingly handsome in a superbly cut white dinner-jacket and narrow black trousers and she was on her way to join him, greeting her mother's guests pleasantly—although she could neither like nor respect them—when she was accosted.

'Annie, dear thing—I swear you're all grown up at last!' This was Jacinth again, overbearing, over-bright, dressed in a plum-coloured and gold caftan, and drawing in tow her languid third husband, a retired interior designer. 'We've all been so worried about darling Willa—quite incommunicado for positively weeks, and rumours about her health flying around like bats!'

Green eyes glittered maliciously and Willa, emerging from an alcove, cut in lightly, 'So naughty of me to worry you all! But, as you see, I'm bursting with disgustingly rude health!' I've simply been selfishly spoiling myself and indulging in a lovely long rest!'

Every head turned, as Willa had intended, and she stretched out her hands, her beautiful, world-famous smile pinned to her face.

The sober blue dress was nowhere to be seen. Willa wore—or almost wore—sleek black satin that might have been moulded to her willowy shape, the halter neckline leaving her back bare, only partially covering milky-white breasts. There were diamonds cascading from her throat and wrists, practically dripping from her fingers, and the silver-blonde candyfloss hair was entrancingly piled on top of her head, a few tendrils escaping to tease her perfect, piquant face and the slender grace of her long, long neck.

From then on the party became something of a nightmare, a recurring nightmare, and Annie could only stand and watch as the replay began.

She had been there before, she had watched the enticing flick of those big brown eyes, the tilt of that beautiful head, the slow drift of impossibly long dark lashes, the inviting smile, the cat-like flick of the tip of a pointed tongue over glossy scarlet lips. She had witnessed Willa give this performance with a dozen different men, and one of them had been Hernando. This time it was Luke.

But this time things were different, she assured herself robustly. Luke loved her, he had said so, and even if he hadn't then his lovemaking, on the sun-warmed sands, would have left her in no doubt. Willa's captivating wiles wouldn't mean a thing to him, and she herself would go and rescue him as soon as she could!

But to her annoyance she found herself surrounded by most of her mother's guests, a dozen people managing to seem like a hundred. It was almost as though they were in collusion with the glittering actress, giving her all the space she needed. She had pinned Luke down in a far corner of the huge room and he was apparently well content with the situation, listening as if spellbound to Willa's obviously sparkling conversation!

Annie banked down the absurd little fires of jealousy and responded as well she could to the questions being lobbed at her from all directions. These people had known her from her schooldays, more used to seeing her as a gangling child hovering in the background. The new Annie, after an absence of seven years, was obviously an eye-opener, and she found that she was being swamped with champagne—the only drink Willa would serve—as her glass was topped up again and again.

As soon as she'd eaten some of the abundant and delicious food she would rescue Luke, she promised herself, trying to edge away from the group without seeming rude. Willa, in this mood and dressed to kill, was totally irresistible. Annie had had too much evidence of this over the years to doubt it now, and although she was far more sure of herself these days she wasn't about to tempt fate!

'So that delicious hunk is your fiancé?' Liz Landor, a watercolourist of remarkable talent and no scruples, enquired breathily as her current escort held a lighter to her thin black cheroot. 'I'd watch it, if I were you, sweetie.' She inhaled deeply and her hoarse voice caught on a snigger. 'We all know no man can resist the divine Willa Kennedy's attentions, and we wouldn't want to see poor little Annie's nose put of out joint again!'

It was a direct reference to the shameful Hernando episode and Annie didn't want publicly reminding of that, thank you very much! Nor did she want her attention drawn to the big seduction scene being so cleverly enacted by her incomparable parent at the other end of the room. She was already too aware of every nuance of that patently scintillating conversation, of every flicker of expertly projected body language, of every movement, every speaking gesture.

But what had happened between her mother and Hernando had happened seven years ago and Annie, drawing herself to her full height, her magnificent eyes glittering with determination, said in deceptively dulcet tones, 'Why don't you all help yourselves to food? I really must go and rescue Luke. I suspect Willa no longer recognises when she's boring the socks off a guy!'

'So long as she only bores his sock off!' Jacinth sniggered again as Annie walked away, furious colour staining her cheeks. On her way across the room, Annie was aware of a dozen pairs of eyes on her back and she deliberately slowed her hectic pace to set down her empty glass on a side-table after recklessly draining the contents. Her perfect teeth were showing in a fixedly bright smile as she edged herself in front of Willa and placed a slim hand on Luke's arm.

'Sorry, Mother, but I'm going to drag Luke away now.' She gave him a too-bright glance. 'I want you to see the garden by moonlight, darling.' Turning to Willa, ignoring her hard look of pique, she observed, 'You're completely neglecting your guests, but don't leave it too long before you go to bed— we don't want you overdoing it again, do we?'

And perhaps that snide remark, coupled with the way she'd separated Willa from her fun, had been a mistake, she thought as she slipped out of the french windows, Luke close behind her. Willa would tolerate such behaviour from no one!

'Your mother's a fascinating woman. And even more beautiful than she appears on screen.' Luke's appreciative voice came from just behind her.

'Isn't she just!' she muttered, and tottered along the terraces, heading for the rose garden.

The night was silky warm, the breeze a mere whisper in the tall dark cypresses, the moonlight a silver caress. A night for romance. But Annie wasn't feeling romantic; she was feeling more than a little intoxicated!

All that carelessly swallowed champagne had left her feeling decidedly odd, she decided as one of her high heels twisted beneath her. She didn't like the feeling of lost control it gave her.

'Hey!' Luke pulled her gently into his arms, one hand cradling her head against his chest, and she melted weakly against him, the inside of her head whirling round and round. 'What's wrong, Annie? Tell me?'

Heard through his chest his voice was a deep warm and comforting rumble and she wanted to stay where she was forever. She couldn't possibly tell him she'd been jealous of her own mother! So she groaned against his shoulder, 'Too much champagne!'

'I noticed.' He held her a little away from him, searching her features with kind eyes, his voice wryly amused as he added, 'You hardly ever drink, do you? But to take too much champagne just once is perfectly excusable. Now, bed for you, sweetheart.'

With a single gentle movement he scooped her up into his arms and carried her back towards the villa. Annie wound her arms around his neck and wanted to cry. So much for their romantic stroll in the moonlight! She felt very ashamed of herself and of the stupid worm of jealousy that had led her to taking all those drinks without noticing what she was doing.

She had been stupid to be even the tiniest bit worried over the effect the magnificent Willa Kennedy was having on Luke. If she hadn't watched the star take Hernando from her, she would have viewed her mother's antics with slightly pitying amusement. Besides, Luke loved her. He had made love to her with passion, but with deep tenderness,

too, and that had to mean something very positive.
And he had told her he loved her and that must
have meant something very much more. And,
loving him in return, she trusted him. He wouldn't
have followed her here if she weren't very special
to him. He wouldn't wreck what they had going
for each other for the sake of one of the short-lived,
tempestuous affairs which Willa considered her
right with any man who turned her on!

Surprising herself, Annie woke early, full of
bounce, with no sign of the headache she so richly
deserved.

Dressing quickly in white cotton jeans and a nut-
brown sleeveless top, she wondered if Luke was up
yet, or whether he was still sleeping in because he'd
been dragged back to the party.

When he'd carried her through the villa last night
he had been careful to avoid being seen by any of
the others. They would have made capital out of
her sorry condition, nothing was surer than that,
so she owed him a big thank-you for that. And for
a whole load of other things, she thought dreamily,
as she dragged a comb through her tumbled hair.
Things such as teaching her to trust again, to love…

The last time she'd seen him had been when he
had gently deposited her on her bed and then
dropped a light but lingering kiss on her lips. He
had disappeared then and moments later Nora had
stumped in, her face resigned.

'Luke tells me you're under the weather,' she'd stated, peering into Annie's flushed face. 'You shouldn't let her get to you.'

She had known what Nora meant, whom she meant, and she had agreed tiredly, wanting nothing more than to be left alone, to curl up and sleep, just as she was. But Nora had insisted on helping her to undress, hanging her things away in one of the big cupboards before finally leaving.

Annie put her comb down and touched her lips with bronze colour. It was barely six o'clock and she was going to make a pot of tea. She would drink it on the patio and dream a little. The details of her future and Luke's was something they were going to have to sort out later, when they'd left the villa—which would be this morning, if Annie had any say in the matter. But for now she could spin a few delicious daydreams all of her own!

Walking silently along the corridor, her footsteps were muffled by the thick silky carpet. Blithely, she nipped around a corner then froze back against the wall, her heart slamming to a painful halt.

Luke, barefoot, was emerging from Willa's bedroom. He turned slowly in the doorway, his back to her, his impressive masculine body naked save for a towel slung low on lean hips.

The villa was hushed, with not even the servants stirring yet, and although his voice was lowered she could hear every word. Every betraying word.

'Don't worry, I'll break the news to Annie myself, if that's what you'd prefer. I'll tell her exactly what's happened.'

'I know it's cowardly, but yes, I would rather she heard it from you.' Willa's voice came breathlessly. 'Her opinion of me is already rock-bottom——'

'It will be all right,' he assured her huskily. Willa had stepped beyond the shelter of her doorway, languorously lovely in a négligé that was little more than a cascade of black lace. Tentatively almost, she placed a white, scarlet-tipped hand against the tanned breadth of his chest and he lifted it to his lips. 'I promise, everything will be fine.' His voice took on a growl of humour that turned Annie sick. 'I know exactly how to deal with your daughter if she makes the unholy fuss you're afraid of!'

'Truly? I shudder to think of what she'll say and do when she discovers——' Willa lifted her perfect profile and, utterly sickened, her blood rushing in painful surges through her veins, Annie watched as Luke bent to drop a kiss on the smooth pale forehead.

Terrified of being discovered, of having them witness her distress, Annie pressed a hand to her racing heart, her mouth dry, as if she had swallowed ashes. But the two in the doorway were oblivious to anything but each other, and when she heard Luke murmur, 'Love takes many forms—Annie will understand—now, go back to bed, you must get some sleep,' she called desperately on all her mental and physical resources and made her way back to her own bedroom on shaky legs.

# CHAPTER TEN

ANNIE didn't slam her door behind her; she closed it very quietly. She was going to handle this thing with dignity—she was left with nothing else but that.

Her initial assessment of Luke's character had been the right one, she told herself grimly, as she folded her clothes into an open suitcase. He was a loner, self-sufficient, he travelled light and made no lasting commitments. And as far as women were concerned he enjoyed the thrill of the chase, the challenge—and, boy, she had been a challenge to his male ego all right! He had even had to say he loved her, and that must have been a first!

Bitterly, she recalled how he'd remarked that he hadn't expected that things would turn out to be so easy. And that had to include her seduction! Just one word of love had been all it had taken, and words were cheap, weren't they? But after the conquest he was running true to form. He simply lost interest and turned his attention to new quarry.

He was a man who would take female companionship where it was offered, provided the woman doing the offering was to his sophisticated taste. And Willa was. Oh, yes, Willa at her most enchanting would be to any man's taste! And hadn't the first words he'd spoken to her at that dreadful party said it all? 'Your mother's a fascinating woman.'

Too fascinating to be resisted. Had Willa not been on the scene then Luke might have retained his interest in her for a few more weeks. But Willa had been on the scene, and obviously very willing. All her life Annie had watched men falling at her mother's feet, succumbing to that fatal charm. Why should Luke be any different? And hadn't she been warned that this very thing could happen?

She had been every kind of fool, she admitted miserably. But his timing had been perfect. He had arrived just as she had realised she was in love with him. And his own words of love had been all that had been needed to tip the balance, to have her giving herself to him with wanton abandonment. She should have had more sense!

Sometimes she didn't understand herself at all. What kind of woman could fall in love with a man who had openly admitted he was only interested in having an affair? But for some warped reasoning of the heart she had trusted him and what had happened had been predictable. After the chase, the conquest. After that—nothing. It was a typical pattern. He inhabited that shallow world where people looked for instant gratification, took what they wanted by fair means or foul.

Her packing completed, she closed the suitcase with a snap. Now all she had to do was call a taxi. She wasn't running from Luke, not this time, she was walking away from a distasteful situation, and if she happened to bump into him before she left she would tell him, calmly and precisely, just what she thought of him!

But all vestiges of composure left her as, after the briefest of taps, he appeared in her doorway. Her heart fluttered wildly and tears pushed at the back of her eyes.

The towel was slung around his neck now, and his lean and muscular body was attired in brief scarlet swimming-trunks that left very little to the imagination.

'Good morning, sweetheart. Feeling better?' His tone was lazy, very laid-back, but his intense blue eyes were, amazingly, a statement of desire.

Annie tried to inject naked dislike into the stare she gave him back but felt her mouth quiver with nerves, her body ache with jealousy, her heart swell until she thought it would burst with love. Yes, damn it all, with love—even after what had happened!

It would be a long time before she would get him out of her system, she acknowledged with an inner cry of despair. She cursed the day that they had met.

If he had never heard of Monk's Hall, never set foot in Seabourne, then she wouldn't now have been facing the dereliction of heartbreak.

He came further into the room, tossing the towel over the top of a chair, his dark hair rumpled, making her stupid heart lurch because he was too damned attractive. Beautiful.

'You're packed?' He had noticed the suitcase, the bed Annie had already stripped, and he added, unforgivably, 'I promised Willa we'd stay on for at least another few days.'

'Did you?' The colour drained from her face, leaving it ashen, and her body was rigid with the effort of holding her temper in check. Was he planning on having an affair with both of them? He was sick! she railed inwardly, almost hysterical.

But it was difficult to think straight when faced by his devastating near nudity, by his diabolical behaviour, and almost impossible to speak. But she got the question out at last because she had to have his confirmation of what she had seen and heard.

'Were you with Willa last night?'

'I was.' His narrowed eyes met hers squarely, as if he saw nothing wrong in his behaviour, and she dragged in a gasp of searing pain.

'Then you're welcome to stay on here for as long it takes to get tired of each other. I'm leaving,' she stated rawly, her eyes glittering like rain-washed jet. 'And I hope I never see you again. You and she just about deserve each other!'

Willa was welcome to Luke. She hadn't liked the home-truths Annie had come out with, not one little bit, and the way she had spoken to her last night had been the final straw. So Willa had taken her revenge in the only way she knew how, and Luke, damn him, had been more than willing to aid and abet her!

Pointedly, she looked at her wristwatch and moved stiffly towards the door. 'I have a phone call to make,' she told him, her voice stilted with the effort of holding on to her self-control.

But he blocked her path, his eyes grim.

'What is it with you?' he grated, anger showing in the flashing steel of his eyes. 'What's this stuff about Willa? About walking out on me again?' His ruthlessly determined hands caught her upper arms, swinging her round to face him when she would have pushed past him to the open door. 'We've come a long way in a short time, Annie, further than I dared hope,' he ground out, his fingers biting into her cringing flesh, 'given your blind spot on honest-to-God emotion.'

'And is that what you call your little fling with Willa?' she hurled at him, learning that it was possible to love and hate at the same time, hating the instinctive way her treacherous body reacted to the searing nearness of him. '"Honest-to-God emotion"? You make me ill!'

'I don't understand you.' His face was tight. He kicked the door closed with his foot, holding her still, his hard fingers leaving bruises that would last for days.

'Oh, don't you?' she sneered. 'And I thought you were an intelligent man! You admit to spending the night with Willa——'

'I did no such thing!' His voice was a lash of contemptuous fury. He looked as if he could have killed her with his bare hands. 'You asked me if I'd been with Willa last night, and so I had. For about a couple of hours.' His words were clipped, derisive. 'I couldn't sleep, so after tossing and turning for hours I went to the pool for a swim. A short time later your mother appeared. She hadn't been able to sleep, either. We talked, that's all. And, in the mood you're in, I have no intention of enlightening you on the subject matter.' He thrust her from him as though she repelled him. 'And if you can make something squalid out of that, then I don't think I like the way your minds works!' He picked up his towel, draping it around his neck. 'If you can't trust me, Annie, then I don't want to know.' His rejection of her was bitter.

But he paused at the door, his eyes chillingly cold, hauntingly beautiful.

'I've been as gentle with you as I know how, all along the line, and I followed you here because I had to. But even my patience has its limits. If what we had means anything at all to you then you'll take time to think things over. You'll stay here and eat lunch with Willa and me in a civilised manner. And maybe—only maybe—I'll be able to bring myself to talk to you this afternoon. But I don't promise anything will come of it because I'm through chasing you. But I do promise this: if you walk out now you'll never see me again.'

She had been shuddering inside ever since he had left the room, his disgust with her plain to see. His anger had been so real, so shattering. As he had said, his patience had finally run out.

His actions, his words, hadn't been those of a two-timing louse. Stark fury had shown in his eyes when he'd accused her of not trusting him, a cold, rejecting bitterness when he'd finally walked out.

And, whatever the rights or wrongs of the situation, she loved him and without him she would always be lonely. But he had said that without trust he didn't want to know. She hadn't trusted him. She still didn't know if she did. The things he had been saying when he'd left Willa's room hadn't sounded like casual conversation!

But she could have handled things differently had she stopped to think. She could have gone to Luke and calmly and sensibly asked him to explain what she had overheard, what she had seen, not verbally jumped on him with bald accusations. So now she was going to have to confront the two of them, ask them to explain what had been happening. It wasn't something she looked forward to, but it had to be done.

Lunch was the kind of nightmare she never wanted to live through again. Willa was plainly ill at ease, fidgeting restlessly with her cutlery, hardly eating a thing, casting more furtive glances at her wristwatch than she did at the company.

Annie struggled manfully with her asparagus quiche and salad, feeling in disgrace as Luke either ignored her or fixed her with that polished marble stare of his. No eyes had the right to be so chilling, to probe deep into her soul, petrifying it with that frigid gorgon stare. Every muscle in her body seemed to be on fire with the tension that was burning her up, every nerve-end shrieking in raw agony. Had Luke entertained a single shred of his former feeling for her she would have detected it.

That he didn't he was making abundantly clear. And it hurt, dear God, it hurt!

She had to say something now or concede defeat, walk away from Luke and never look back. But she knew she would always be looking back at what might have been, what could have been.

Hiding her shaking hands beneath the table-cloth, she cleared her throat.

'Is one of you going to explain about the news Luke was supposed to break to me?' she asked, her voice tinny. She was hardly aware of Willa's gasp, of the way she dropped her fork to her plate with a clatter that sounded deafening in the suddenly silent room. She was only aware of the strange stillness of Luke's body, of his intent gaze. Flustered, she licked her lips and tried again, 'The gist of the conversation I overheard as Luke left your room, Mother, very early this morning——' She forced herself to look at the actress, thrown off-balance by the look of distress on the older woman's face, but ploughed on doggedly '—had something to do with some unpalatable news Luke was supposed to break.'

'Oh, Luke!' Willa was obviously shaken. 'You haven't——?'

'Told her yet?' Luke put in. 'No. Annie and I have been engaged in quite a different battle.' He dropped his napkin on the table and stood up, helping Willa to her feet. 'Why don't you go and rest? I'll tell Annie all she needs to know.'

Surprisingly, his eyes were soft with a kind of concern, showing nothing of the bitterness that had been there earlier, as he turned to her after escorting Willa to the door.

'You were there when I left after taking Willa back to her room this morning?' he questioned softly and Annie could only nod. What difference did it make? She didn't understand what was going on.

'What you overheard must have seemed pretty damning,' he conceded. 'Shall we take a walk?'

Shying away from his warm glance, she nodded, getting clumsily to her feet, reaching the open french windows before him.

She didn't know how he could explain away what she'd overheard and, suddenly, she was afraid to hear it. He had rejected her this morning because of her lack of trust. Nothing had changed.

Was he about to give her another tongue-lashing for her lack of trust? Was he going to lie to her about what had been happening in Willa's room in the early hours of this morning?

'Luke, I don't need this,' she said thickly. 'You said all there was to say this morning.'

'I said that if you stayed, didn't do another runner, we would talk,' he reminded softly.

'You said maybe,' she corrected acidly, a sudden unlooked-for spurt of anger sending adrenalin rushing through her veins. She turned, her eyes bright, filled with unshed tears. 'But *maybe*,' she stressed, 'I think enough has been said.'

'Annie!' Her name, on his lips, was a sigh wrenched from his soul. 'How could you not have trusted me after the beautiful thing we shared? I

know the evidence of your eyes and ears must have
been damning, but at least you could have asked
me. Your lack of trust was something I simply
couldn't cope with.'

They had reached the shore now, almost without
her being aware of it, and tears stung her eyes as
she remembered the beauty of his lovemaking, here
on this very spot. And tears blurred her vision,
breaking the smooth surface of the sea into a
million dancing lights.

'How could you believe me to be the type of man
to make love to you in the afternoon and ravish
your damned mother at night? I may not be a saint,
but I'm not a bloody tomcat!'

'I know.' Every last trace of anger left her. She
did know now, when it was probably far too late.
She had been defeated by her own idiocy. 'But I
had my reasons.'

'Then *tell* me,' he demanded thickly. 'I can think
of no reason on God's sweet earth that could make
you believe I'd spent the night making love to Willa.
She's a beautiful woman but, damn it all, Annie—
I was in love with you.'

'Was' being the operative word, she thought
dully, watching as he began restlessly to pace the
sand.

'I loved you more than I loved my pride,' he
grated, whirling back to face her, the breadth of
his chest heaving with suppressed emotion. 'Otherwise I would have given up on you when you walked
out on me back in England. So tell me,' he commanded, his mouth a grim slash, 'why couldn't you

have asked for my side of the story before jumping to all those hateful conclusions?'

She shook her head. What was the use? He was angry, bitter, as he probably had every right to be. But, on his own admission, the love he'd had for her had died. So what was the point of saying anything?

'Annie——' his hands fastened on her shoulders, the pressure of his fingers turning her flesh to fire '—I have never spanked a woman in my life. Don't make me do it now.'

His voice was gruff, as if he meant every word, and the bittersweet pressure of his hands increased as he ground out, 'You're a miser with yourself. You keep something hidden, locked away. I've always known that, faced it, but I thought I could get you to trust me, to let me reach you. Don't tell me I was wrong!'

Suddenly, he dragged her to him with a smothered groan, gathering her into his arms, his cheeks warm against the tears that had been falling unheeded.

She felt his hurt, matching her own, and she blurted out, 'Willa has always had to be first, the centre of all attention. If she saw a man she wanted she went right ahead and took him, never mind who got hurt. And it was always easy for her—so damned easy!' She had never spoken of her earlier life with Willa to anyone. Willa was public property, a legend, and Annie was loyal. But no loyalty—nothing—mattered now.

She flung away from him, kicking off her shoes, walking rapidly to the distant line of water, driven to restless movement by the anguish inside her.

And Luke was right beside her, his hand on her arm.

'There has to be more.'

'Oh, there's more,' she rapped out bitterly, dragging her arm from his grasp, turning, heading back the way she had come. 'But I can't believe you're interested!' How could he be, when her lack of trust had killed his love?

'For God's sake, Annie!' he exclaimed huskily, hauling her back into his arms, holding her tightly against his body. 'Don't clam up on me now.' His hands began to move along her back, soothing away the tension, gentling her, and she shuddered, releasing a shaky breath. Maybe he still cared for her, after all.

'So tell me, my darling,' he whispered, his lips just touching the corner of hers, and she submitted completely, knowing that he would always have this effect on her, his slightest touch melting her, making her defenceless.

Haltingly at first, but then with more confidence, she told him of Willa's various husbands, of how they'd lasted only marginally longer than her lovers. She told him of Hernando, and how easily Willa had taken him from her.

'And when I arrived here I found Willa in one of her states,' she confided, 'I told her a few home-truths, which she couldn't have liked and when I saw you coming out of her room, heard the things you were saying to her, I thought she had taken her revenge in the way she knows best.'

'I see.' His hands travelled slowly across her back to her shoulders, lingering at the base of her neck before idling upwards to cup her face, tilting her head to look deep into her eyes.

For a rapturous moment she thought he was going to kiss her, and she needed that kiss with every atom of her being, but he said thoughtfully, 'Will you believe me if I tell you that nothing happened between me and Willa last night? That the kiss you saw me give her was my way of comforting her, of reassuring her that everything would be all right?'

The deep blue eyes held hers for what seemed like an eternity and she felt relief, an aching sadness. She had wrongly imputed to her beloved Luke the type of shallowness Norman had hinted so strongly at, the shallowness of the people who had surrounded her while she was growing up. And she had been wrong, so wrong. She would believe him unreservedly, whatever he said.

'Of course. Utterly,' she whispered, her head drooping forward on the slender column of her neck, resting against his chest, feeling his warmth, breathing in the spicy male muskiness of him.

'Thank God!' There was more than mere relief in his voice as his arms enclosed her more firmly. Then, lowering them both to the sand, he told her huskily, 'As I told you, my love, I couldn't sleep last night. Knowing you were under the same roof made me restless as hell! I went to swim in the pool and Willa appeared, clearly distressed. She hadn't been able to sleep, either, for worrying over how she was going to break the news to you.'

'What news?' Annie wasn't much interested now; her hand was walking across his chest, finding the buttons of his shirt, her fingers slipping beneath the silky fabric, and she heard his breath catch in a highly satisfactory way before he captured her errant hand and held it tightly in his own.

'The news that she has decided to mend her ways,' he told her in a voice that suggested he was having trouble with his breathing. 'She'd had a disastrous affair with a man much younger than herself, apparently, and had been mooching around, trying to decide what to do with herself in the future. In her own words, she couldn't go on as she had been doing. She was not getting any younger and had a hankering for a secure, long-term relationship. The upshot was, she's decided to accept her agent's proposal. This Griff guy has been in love with her for years, so she said. But she knew how well you and he had always got along and she was afraid that, knowing her track record, you might scratch her eyes out before you'd let her treat him as she's treated all the others.'

Annie had grown very still in his arms and now she said doubtfully, 'Do you think she means it? About wanting a long-term relationship?' Fond as she was of Griff, she was fonder of her mother. And nothing would give her greater pleasure than to see her settle down to a normal, loving marriage.

And Luke whispered against her hair, 'I think so. Anyway, I promised to break the news. Willa's been like a cat on hot bricks all day, waiting for him to arrive, for your reaction. But whatever happens in that quarter is in the lap of the gods. What is not——' his fingers curled gently around her neck '—in the lap of the gods is our future. You'll never walk away from me again, even if I have to keep you chained to my side! I love you, my darling. It began the moment I first saw you and it's never going to end. I think I must have loved you always, because right now I can't remember a moment when I didn't.'

Annie grew very still, hardly daring to breathe as she lay in his arms, their legs entwined, her hands spread against his chest, feeling the steady beat of his heart.

'You said you didn't want to know—not if I didn't trust you,' she reminded wickedly, her fingers finding a life of their own, shamelessly stroking the hard wall of his chest, feeling the low rumble of laughter leave his lungs.

'But you came up trumps in the end, didn't you?' he almost gloated. 'And I know what I said, and at the time I couldn't cope with your lack of trust. But I would never have given up on you, not even if I'd had to chase after you for the rest of my life— which would have been hellish frustrating, not to mention tiring!' His lips nuzzled the vulnerable spot below her earlobe, the moist, erotic pressure sending tremors of wildfire through every vein, every pulse-beat. Smiling, he took the tip of her finger into his mouth, his exploring tongue making her body melt with rapture, then gently, tormentingly, he nibbled until she thought she might die of the pleasure he was already giving, deciding she'd probably fragment into a million pieces if he took his love-making further.

Then he lifted his head, his magnificent eyes dancing with love-lights.

'We'll be married as soon as it can be arranged, and that means reneging on the promise I made to Willa—for both of us. We'll get back to England right away and make arrangements for the ceremony.'

'Are you asking, or telling?' She smiled wickedly, her heart just about bursting with her love for him, and Luke lay back on the sand, his arms crossed behind him, the golden rays of the sunlight making his features even more heart-stoppingly handsome.

'Telling,' he said succinctly. 'I aim to do all the telling in our marriage—you're such a contrary creature that if I gave you your head you'd have us both running in circles, getting nowhere.'

'Not any more,' she whispered. Life with this dynamic man was going to be exciting, blissful, poignantly beautiful—all those things and more besides.

'Thank the lord for that!' he grinned, reaching up to pull her down beside him. 'And just to set the record straight, about Monk's Hall——'

'Luke, it doesn't matter,' she cut him short, burying her head in his shoulder. 'You can turn it into a glue factory for all I care,' she assured him, meaning it.

He said lazily, 'I think the good citizens of Seabourne might have something to say about that! No, my sweet, I have something entirely different in mind for that house.' Idly, his fingers wandered through the silky fire of her hair and she curled her body closer to his. 'I fell in love with a girl and a house on the same day and decided I was going to have both. All my ideas for a hotel flew out of the window—Monk's Hall meant far more to me than a money-making proposition. As far as I was concerned it was our future home, but you came along and pushed the bidding sky-high! Still...' He ran a reflective finger over the curve of her cheek, bringing it slowly to rest on the full curve of her lips. 'It was worth every penny and at that stage of the game I couldn't tell you it was to be our home, or you'd have punched me in the eye, but I did tell Norman.'

'You did?' Norman's snide remarks about his cousin were beginning to fall into place. 'When?'

'As soon as I realised that you didn't love each other, that your marriage would have been one of convenience. I gave him fair warning——' He broke off, her hands having wandered inside his shirt, as if they had a life of their own. He grunted, his fingers busy with the tiny buttons of her top. 'We've talked far too much,' he warned her thickly. 'We have other things to occupy us.'

'Such as?' she enquired dulcetly, her heart beginning to pound, totally out of control now as he exposed one lace-covered breast and then the other.

'How to manipulate the strange but adorable items of apparel you seem to find necessary,' he explained as if he had some terrible grievance, his fingertips teasing her taut nipples through the gossamer lace, and Annie smiled dreamily, her whole body aching for the delight they would soon give each other.

'Don't overtax yourself, darling, let me show you . . .'

It was almost twilight when they walked slowly back to the villa, leaning against each other, their arms entwined. Luke had made love to her until she'd been reeling with the wonder of it, and he had taught her how to please him and that would be a lesson she would never forget. And now, almost too sated to put one foot in front of the other, she frowned as she heard the rumble of an engine coming up the drive, approaching the villa.

'That's got to be Griff,' Annie told Luke, nuzzling her head deeper into his shoulder as the car drew to a halt and a burly grey-haired man emerged. 'Better late than never.'

'And that's a taxi, right?' Luke was fully alert now, dragging her behind him as he loped over the terraces.

'Annie, baby—good to see you!' her mother's agent greeted. 'Sorry to be so late, but——'

'I'm glad you could make it at all,' Annie assured him as Luke left her side, going to poke his head in through the open taxi window.

'How's Willa?' the genial giant enquired, his eyes shrewd and watchful.

'She's——' Annie lifted her shoulders, spreading her hands, grinning. 'She's Willa.'

'Says it all, baby.' He picked up his case, turning to smile at Luke as he loped back from the cab, and Annie introduced them, knowing instinctively that the two men would be friends, hoping quite desperately that Willa would find long-term happiness with the man who had silently adored her for years.

'Well, I guess I ought to track my hostess down,' Griff was saying. 'I have a very personal matter to discuss with that lady, but see you guys at supper.'

'Not if I have any say in the matter,' Luke responded with a grin. 'Nothing personal, Griff, but this lady and I need a slice of privacy.' His smile took any sting out of his words.

Annie added quickly, 'Griff—tell Willa I'll dance at her wedding. Tell her to be happy. She'll know what I mean.'

'Will do.' His heavy brows lowered for a moment before he pulled himself together, and disappeared into the house, his intention to find his beloved accelerated by Annie's words.

'The driver's going to wait,' Luke told her gently, his words muffled through the kiss he placed on her parted lips.

'For us?' she murmured, her tongue playing with his sensual lower lip.

'Don't do that!' he groaned. 'Unless you want me to make love to you in front of one highly interested Italian cabbie! Now.' He held her a little away from him, smiling down into her desire-hazed eyes. 'Can you pack in three minutes?'

'Two, if I have to.'

'Good girl!' He swung her round and patted her neat bottom. 'Get moving. We'll be out of here in five minutes flat, on our way to start renovating a highly desirable property back home. Unless, of course, you have any fond and lingering farewells to make?'

'Not one.' As far as she was concerned the past was a blank page, and the future, her future and Luke's, lay enticingly ahead. And it began right now.

*Back by Popular Demand*

# Janet Dailey
## Americana

A romantic tour of America through fifty favorite Harlequin
Presents, each set in a different state researched by Janet
and her husband, Bill. A journey of a lifetime in one
cherished collection.

In August, don't miss the exciting states featured in:

Title #13 — ILLINOIS
   The Lyon's Share

 #14 — INDIANA
   The Indy Man

*Available wherever
Harlequin books are sold.*

You'll flip . . . your pages won't!
Read paperbacks *hands-free* with

# Book Mate・I

**The perfect "mate" for all your romance paperbacks**

**Traveling • Vacationing • At Work • In Bed • Studying
• Cooking • Eating**

Perfect size for all standard paperbacks, this wonderful invention makes reading a pure pleasure! Ingenious design holds paperback books OPEN and FLAT so even wind can't ruffle pages — leaves your hands free to do other things. Reinforced, wipe-clean vinyl-covered holder flexes to let you turn pages without undoing the strap . . . supports paperbacks so well, they have the strength of hardcovers!

Pages turn WITHOUT opening the strap

SEE-THROUGH STRAP

Reinforced back stays flat

Built in bookmark

BOOK MARK

BACK COVER HOLDING STRIP

10 x 7¼ opened
Snaps closed for easy carrying, too

This August, don't miss an exclusive
two-in-one collection of earlier love stories

# MAN
# WITH A PAST

---

# TRUE COLORS

### by one of today's hottest
### romance authors,

Now, two of Jayne Ann Krentz's most loved books are
available together in this special edition that new and
longtime fans will want to add to their bookshelves.

Let Jayne Ann Krentz capture your hearts with the love
stories, MAN WITH A PAST and TRUE COLORS.

And in October, watch for the second two-in-one
collection by Barbara Delinsky!

Available wherever Harlequin books are sold.